SOPHOMORE SOLSTICE
A PARANORMAL HOLIDAY ROMANCE

NORTH POLE UNIVERSITY
BOOK TWO

MARIE-HELENE LEBEAULT

BEACHES AND TRAILS
PUBLISHING

CHAPTER ONE

PRANKS AND PRESSURE

DYLAN

The thing about being a fox shifter at North Pole University is that everyone expects you to be clever. The problem with being a *Vixen* fox shifter is that everyone expects you to be clever *and* charming *and* naturally gifted at getting out of trouble.

I was currently batting zero for three.

"Mr. Vixen," Professor Blitzen's voice cut through the morning air like a sleigh blade through fresh powder, "would you care to explain why the Frost Hall's gargoyles are currently singing show tunes?"

I glanced up at the carved ice creatures perched along the building's Gothic arches. Sure enough, they were belting out what sounded suspiciously like "Defying Gravity" in perfect four-part harmony. Their stone voices echoed across the courtyard, drawing amused glances from passing students and making the nearby snow sprites giggle.

Definitely my handiwork. Though I couldn't remember the spell lasting this long. More unsettling was the way my fox senses were picking up something off about the magic itself—like the scent of ozone before a storm, sharp and electric in a way that made the hair on the back of my neck prickle. Illusion magic wasn't supposed to smell like that.

"Well, Professor," I said, flashing my most disarming grin— the one that had gotten me out of detention approximately seventeen times last year, "I think they're just expressing their artistic freedom. Who are we to stifle their creative voices?"

A few students snickered. Professor Blitzen was not amused.

Her antlers—perfectly maintained and decorated with tiny silver bells that chimed when she was particularly irritated— were practically vibrating. As head of the Reindeer Games preparation committee, she took campus disruptions about as well as Santa took coal requests.

"Detention, Mr. Vixen. After classes. You'll be polishing sleigh runners until those gargoyles return to their appropriately stoic silence."

"But Professor, I have—"

"*Two* detentions if you finish that sentence."

I wisely snapped my mouth shut, though I caught Finn MacTiernan—a fellow fox shifter from my year—shaking his head at me from across the courtyard. His expression clearly said *when will you learn?*

The answer, apparently, was not today.

As Professor Blitzen clip-clopped away, her hooves striking the enchanted cobblestones with sharp disapproval, I slumped against the fountain at the courtyard's center. The carved ice dolphins swimming through the frozen water seemed to be smirking at me.

"Smooth, Vixen. Really smooth."

I looked up to find Kieran Frost—no relation to the newly-revealed Prince Elian, just unfortunate naming—lounging against a nearby lamp post. As a winter wolf shifter, he had that effort-lessly cool demeanor that I'd been trying to perfect for years. His pale hair caught the morning light, and his silver eyes held just enough amusement to be insulting.

"Says the guy who got caught putting itching powder in the polar bear shifters' practice gear last month," I shot back.

"Yeah, but I didn't get *caught*. There's an art to it, Dylan. You're supposed to be the trickster here."

That stung more than it should have. Kieran was right—fox shifters were legendary for our cleverness, our ability to slip out of consequences with wit and charm. My older brothers had perfected it to an art form. Hell, my *father* was still telling stories about his university pranks forty years later.

So why did I feel like I was constantly swimming upstream?

"Besides," Kieran continued, checking his reflection in the fountain's surface, "aren't you supposed to be focusing on acade-mics this year? You said your parents gave you the whole 'shape up or else' speech over summer break."

My stomach clenched. He wasn't wrong. The conversation with my parents had been... uncomfortable. Three generations of Vixen fox shifters had graduated with honors from NPU. They'd all gone on to prestigious positions in the North Pole's magical government, diplomatic corps, or elite courier services. They were clever, successful, and absolutely baffled by their youngest son's academic mediocrity.

"Dylan, darling," my mother had said in that perfectly controlled voice she used when she was disappointed, *"your first-year grades were... concerning. Perhaps it's time you applied yourself with more... focus."*

My father had been more direct: *"Son, the Reindeer Games are in the spring. If you want to participate—if you want to prove you belong with the elite shifter houses—you need to show you're worthy of the Vixen name."*

No pressure or anything.

The thing was, I *wanted* to make the team. Not just for them, but for me. If I made the Reindeer Games roster, I'd get more than bragging rights—I'd finally prove I was more than just the screw-up Vixen kid. The one who couldn't live up to the family legacy of cunning brilliance. Maybe then this constant feeling of being one step behind, one trick short, would finally go away.

"I'm handling it," I told Kieran, which wasn't entirely a lie. I *was* handling it. Just... not very well.

"Right. Well, good luck with that detention." Kieran pushed off from the lamp post with fluid grace. "Try not to enchant anything else today, yeah? Some of us actually need to study."

As he walked away, I caught sight of my reflection in the fountain and grimaced. My rust-colored hair was doing that thing where it stuck up at odd angles, and there were bags under my green eyes that spoke to too many late nights spent cramming for exams I'd inevitably bomb anyway.

I looked tired. More than that, I looked... ordinary.

The thought made something uncomfortable twist in my chest. It wasn't that I wasn't trying. I'd read half a textbook last night—okay, skimmed, but that had to count for something, right? Maybe I was just pushing too hard, trying to force cleverness instead of letting it flow naturally.

I pushed the doubt down and checked my class schedule, scrawled on a piece of enchanted parchment that updated itself throughout the day. Next up: Advanced Illusion Theory with Professor Mistral.

Perfect. Maybe I could redeem myself with some actual academic participation.

I was halfway across the courtyard when I felt it—that weird flutter in my chest that usually preceded a shift. But I wasn't trying to shift. Hell, I wasn't even thinking about my fox form.

Odd.

I paused by the Frost Hall steps, pressing a hand to my sternum. The feeling intensified for a moment, like something was trying to claw its way out from the inside, then faded completely. When I pulled my hand away, I could swear I saw the faintest shimmer of russet fur across my knuckles before it disappeared.

My fox form had never tried to surface on its own before.

Definitely odd.

"Dylan!"

I turned to see Tobias Reindeer jogging toward me, his breath creating small clouds in the crisp morning air. As one of the legacy reindeer shifters, Toby had been selected for advanced Reindeer Games training since our first week of freshman year. He was good-natured about it, but there was no ignoring the gulf between students like him and students like... well, me.

"Hey, Toby. What's up?"

"Did you hear? They're posting the preliminary Games roster today." His brown eyes sparkled with excitement. "Coach Prancer wants to see you after lunch."

My heart did a complicated dance somewhere between hope and terror. "Me? Are you sure?"

"Positive. She specifically asked for Dylan Vixen." Toby grinned. "Looks like someone's making good on those summer promises."

After he bounded away—literally bounded, with the easy grace of someone whose animal form was built for leaping—I stood alone on the steps, processing this information.

Coach Prancer wanted to see me. About the Reindeer Games.

The Reindeer Games weren't just NPU's most prestigious competition—they were a direct pipeline to the magical elite. Winning teams got fast-tracked into the best internships, the most exclusive magical societies, the kinds of positions that came with corner offices and invitations to solstice galas.

More importantly, they were a chance to prove I belonged here. A chance to show everyone—including myself—that Dylan Vixen was more than just a pretty face and a clever tongue.

The weird feeling in my chest stirred again, fainter this time, like an echo of something not quite right. Along with it came that strange ozone scent, stronger now, mixed with something that reminded me of burnt copper.

I shook my head, trying to clear it. Probably just nerves about the Games meeting.

Right. Because nothing says 'team material' like a fox shifter whose magic smells like electrical fire.

Time to show everyone what I could really do.

I just hoped I actually knew what that was.

———

By the time I slid into my seat in Professor Mistral's Advanced Illusion Theory classroom, the gargoyles had moved on to what sounded like a medley from *Les Misérables*. Their stone voices carried through the tall windows, providing an oddly dramatic soundtrack to the morning's lesson on "Sustainable Illusion Magic: Theory and Practice."

Professor Mistral—an elegant snow elf with silver hair that seemed to move in a perpetual, gentle breeze—was already writing complex magical equations on the blackboard. The chalk moved of its own accord, guided by subtle gestures from her long fingers.

"Ah, Mr. Vixen," she said without turning around. "How good of you to join us. I trust the Frost Hall gargoyles' newfound vocal talents aren't too distracting?"

A few students chuckled. I felt heat creep up my neck.

"Not at all, Professor. I find music helps with concentration."

"Wonderful. Then perhaps you can concentrate long enough to explain the fundamental difference between temporary illusion magic and sustained enchantment."

I opened my mouth, then closed it. Around me, other students were pulling out notebooks and quills, settling in for what was clearly going to be an interrogation session. At the desk next to mine, a water sprite named Coral was already scribbling notes, her blue-tinted fingers moving with practiced efficiency.

"The difference is..." I started, then paused. I *knew* this. We'd covered it last semester. "Temporary illusions rely on the caster's active magical focus, while sustained enchantments are anchored to objects or locations using stored magical energy?"

"Correct. And can you tell me why this matters for practical application?"

"Because..." Another pause. The weird flutter in my chest was back, stronger now. It felt almost like my fox form was trying to surface, but wrong somehow. Disconnected. "Because if you want an illusion to last longer than your concentration span, you need to anchor it properly or it'll... fade unpredictably?"

"Precisely. Which brings us to today's lesson on magical sustainability and the importance of understanding your own limitations." Her pale eyes fixed on me with laser focus. "Mr. Vixen, given your... extracurricular activities this morning, you'll be our demonstration volunteer."

Oh, fantastic.

Professor Mistral gestured, and a small golden orb appeared floating above her palm. "I want you to create a simple illusion—

nothing elaborate, just alter the orb's color—and maintain it for sixty seconds."

Simple enough. I'd been doing basic illusions since I was twelve.

I closed my eyes, reaching for that familiar sensation of magical energy pooling in my core. Fox shifter magic was all about misdirection and transformation—making things appear different than they actually were. It should have felt as natural as breathing.

Instead, it felt like trying to grab smoke.

I furrowed my brow, concentrating harder. The magic was there, I could sense it, but every time I tried to direct it toward the floating orb, it slipped away from me like water through cupped hands.

"Mr. Vixen?" Professor Mistral's voice sounded concerned now rather than challenging.

"I'm... just give me a second." Sweat beaded on my forehead despite the classroom's cool temperature. Come on, Dylan. Basic illusion magic. You've done this a thousand times.

Finally, *finally*, I managed to grasp a thread of magical energy and direct it toward the orb. It flickered from gold to deep green—my signature color—for about three seconds before snapping back to its original state.

The snap back hurt. Not physically, but like something had been yanked away from me mid-reach. The taste of copper flooded my mouth, and for a moment, the edges of my vision went fuzzy.

The classroom was very quiet.

"Interesting," Professor Mistral murmured, reaching toward the space where the orb had been floating. She paused for a fraction of a second, her pale fingers hovering in the air as if she could

feel something lingering there—some trace of the magical wrong-
ness that had just occurred. Then she seemed to shake herself and
dismissed the remaining traces of the spell with a wave of her
hand. "Class, please read chapter twelve for tomorrow. We'll
discuss magical fatigue and its effects on spellcasting."

As students began filing out, chattering quietly among themselves, I remained frozen in my seat. Magical fatigue? I wasn't
tired. I'd gotten plenty of sleep last night.

So why had that simple spell felt like trying to lift a boulder
with my bare hands?

"Ugh, I can't believe Professor Ember assigned another essay
already," Coral muttered as she packed up her things. "I was
hoping to get some tutoring help this week, but I heard the
Lumina girl's schedule is completely full. Again."

The water sprite's complaint barely registered as I tried to
process what had just happened to my magic.

"Mr. Vixen, a word?"

I approached Professor Mistral's desk on unsteady legs. She
was organizing her notes with the same fluid grace she brought to
everything else, but her expression was thoughtful.

"Dylan, have you been experiencing any... irregularities with
your magic lately?"

"Define irregularities."

"Spells not working as expected. Magical energy feeling different. Perhaps issues with your shifting abilities?"

The question hit too close to home. I thought about the weird
flutter in my chest, the way my shift had felt off during this morning's prank, the ozone scent that had been following me around
like a bad omen.

"Maybe," I admitted reluctantly. "But it's probably just stress,
right? About the Games and grades, and everything?"

Professor Mistral nodded slowly. "Possibly. Stress can certainly affect magical performance. However..." She paused, studying me with those pale, perceptive eyes. "I think it would be wise for you to schedule an appointment with the Magical Health Center. Just as a precautionary measure."

"Is that really necessary? I mean, it's probably nothing—"

"Dylan." Her voice was gentle but firm. "You're a talented young man with considerable potential. But magic is not something to take chances with. Promise me you'll make that appointment."

I nodded, even though every instinct was screaming at me to downplay this, to brush it off as a temporary glitch that would resolve itself.

As I gathered my books and headed for the door, Professor Mistral called after me.

"And Dylan? Perhaps... limit the pranks for a while. Until we know what's going on."

I forced a smile. "Where's the fun in that, Professor?"

But as I walked through the halls of Frost Hall, the gargoyles still singing their hearts out above, I couldn't shake the feeling that something fundamental had shifted.

And not in a good way.

The gargoyles hit a particularly high note that seemed to vibrate through the stone itself. As their voices soared, I heard something crack—sharp and clean, like ice splitting. Through the tall windows, I could see the courtyard fountain, and sure enough, a thin fracture had appeared right down the center of the carved ice dolphins.

Coincidence, I told myself. *Had to be.*

But as I watched, the crack spread wider, and I couldn't help but think it looked a little too much like the jagged feeling currently taking up residence in my chest.

The question was: what was I going to do about it?

More importantly, what if there was nothing I *could* do about it?

And most terrifying of all: what if whatever was wrong with me was just getting started?

CHAPTER TWO
LYRA'S LIGHT

LYRA

The Light Observatory at dawn was the closest thing to perfection I'd found at North Pole University.

Perched atop the Lumina Wing like a crystalline crown, the circular chamber was designed to capture and amplify natural magical illumination. Aurora light streamed through the transparent dome overhead, painting everything in shifting hues of green and gold. The constellation maps embedded in the walls pulsed gently, tracking celestial movements with mathematical precision that made my heart sing.

Here, surrounded by the organized beauty of light magic theory, I could almost forget that most of my fellow students found me as cold and untouchable as the ice sculptures in the courtyard below.

I adjusted the focus on my luminescence spectrometer, watching the readout stabilize at exactly the parameters I'd calculated the night before. Perfect. The aurora patterns this semester were ideal for my advanced thesis on "Sustained Light Magic in Seasonal Environments"—a project that would hopefully secure my position as Professor Lumina's research assistant next year.

Assuming I could maintain my current academic standing. Assuming no distractions interfered with my carefully structured schedule. Assuming—

A soft chime from my enchanted planner interrupted my spiraling thoughts. New appointment request. I sighed, already knowing what I'd find when I checked it.

Another tutoring request.

The holographic display showed a list that had grown depressingly long since the semester began: "Struggling with Elemental Theory basics," "Need help with Light Magic fundamentals," "Desperate—failing Advanced Magical Mathematics." Each request represented another student who saw me as a solution to their academic problems rather than, well, a person.

Not that I was particularly good at the person part anyway.

Sometimes I wondered if people avoided me because I made them uncomfortable... or because I preferred it that way. I wasn't sure which answer bothered me more.

I scrolled through the messages with practiced efficiency, mentally calculating how many hours each request would require and whether I could fit them into my schedule without compromising my own research. The math was becoming impossible. There weren't enough hours in the day, even with my perfectly optimized study routine.

My finger paused over the newest entry, submitted just this morning: "Dylan Vixen - Illusion Magic assistance needed. Urgent."

Dylan Vixen. The name stirred a vague memory. Fox shifter, wasn't he? One of the popular crowd who moved through NPU's social circles with the easy confidence I'd never managed to master. I was fairly certain I'd seen him around campus—rust-colored hair, green eyes, usually laughing about something with his friends.

Why would someone like him need someone like me?

I pulled up his academic record with a few quick gestures. The holographic display painted a picture that made me frown: middling grades across the board, several disciplinary notices for "creative magical applications" (a diplomatic way of saying pranks), and concerning notes from multiple professors about inconsistent magical performance.

Interesting. Not the typical profile of someone who sought out advanced tutoring. Most of my usual clients were overachievers pushing for perfect marks or struggling students desperate to avoid failing. Dylan Vixen appeared to be something else entirely—someone coasting in the middle, suddenly needing help.

The fact that his request was marked "urgent" suggested something had changed recently.

I was still contemplating this puzzle when the Observatory's main door chimed, admitting my guardian in a swirl of silver robes and barely contained academic intensity.

"Good morning, Lyra." Professor Lumina's voice carried the same precise articulation that had shaped my own speaking patterns since childhood. Her pale blonde hair was pulled back in its customary elegant twist, and her ice-blue eyes immediately took in the experiment setup with approving efficiency. "I see you're making excellent progress with the seasonal light variance study."

"The preliminary data is promising," I replied, pulling up my charts with a gesture. "The aurora patterns this year show 23% more consistency than last semester's readings, which should provide a cleaner baseline for the sustainability calculations."

Professor Lumina nodded, moving to examine my work with

the keen attention that had made her one of NPU's most respected researchers. She wasn't technically my mother—I'd been placed in her care as an infant through circumstances I'd never fully understood—but she'd raised me with the same dedication she brought to her magical studies.

Which was to say: with high expectations and very little patience for anything less than excellence.

"Excellent work, as always." She paused, and I caught the subtle shift in her expression that meant she had something else on her mind. "I understand you've received quite a few tutoring requests this semester."

It wasn't really a question. Professor Lumina made it her business to know everything that might affect my academic performance.

"Yes, ma'am. Perhaps more than I can reasonably accommodate without compromising my research schedule."

"Hmm." She moved to the eastern window, gazing out at the campus below, where early morning students were beginning to emerge from the dormitories. "You know, Lyra, there's something to be said for... broadening one's horizons. Engaging with different types of students can provide a valuable perspective on magical theory applications."

I blinked, surprised. Professor Lumina rarely encouraged activities that might distract from my studies. "Are you suggesting I should accept more tutoring appointments?"

"I'm suggesting," she said carefully, "that perhaps you might consider working with students who present... unique challenges. Sometimes the most interesting discoveries come from examining problems we haven't encountered before."

Her tone had that particular quality that meant she had someone specific in mind.

"Is there a particular student you think I should work with?"

Professor Lumina's smile was enigmatic. "I believe a Mr. Dylan Vixen submitted a request this morning. His situation might prove... educationally illuminating."

Dylan Vixen. So this wasn't a coincidence.

"Professor, may I ask why you're specifically interested in this student?"

"Let's just say that his recent magical difficulties have come to the attention of several faculty members. Professor Mistral mentioned some concerning inconsistencies in his spellwork." She turned from the window, fixing me with that steady gaze that missed nothing. "I thought perhaps a tutor with your particular expertise in magical theory might be able to help identify the underlying issues."

Translation: they suspected there was more to Dylan Vixen's academic troubles than simple laziness, and they wanted me to figure out what.

Part of me bristled at being volunteered as an unofficial magical diagnostician. I had my own research to focus on, my own academic goals to pursue. I didn't have time to solve mysterious magical problems for popular fox shifters who'd probably never spoken to me in two years of shared classes.

But another part of me—the part that had been raised on the intellectual challenge of solving complex magical puzzles—was undeniably intrigued.

"I suppose I could fit him into my schedule," I said carefully. "If it's truly important for his academic progress."

"Excellent." Professor Lumina's smile widened slightly. "I'll let the administration know you've accepted the appointment. Oh, and Lyra?"

"Yes, ma'am?"

"Remember that sometimes the most valuable lessons come from the students we don't expect to learn from."

After she left, I stood alone in the Observatory, watching the aurora light shift across my carefully organized research stations. Professor Lumina's words echoed in my mind, mixing with my curiosity about Dylan Vixen's "urgent" need for tutoring help.

What could have changed so suddenly for him?

I pulled up his request again, reading between the lines of the brief message. Most tutoring requests came with detailed explanations of specific topics or upcoming exams. His was strangely vague, almost as if he wasn't entirely sure what he needed help with.

Or as if he was too proud to admit the full extent of the problem.

Typical fox shifter, I thought with a slight shake of my head. *Too charming for their own good, too proud to ask for help until it's almost too late.*

Still, Professor Lumina was rarely wrong about these things. If she thought Dylan Vixen's situation was worth my attention, there had to be more to it than simple academic struggling.

I made a note in my planner to send him a meeting time, then turned back to my aurora variance calculations. But I found my attention drifting, part of my mind already analyzing the puzzle he represented.

Dylan Vixen. Popular, confident, magically gifted enough to pull off elaborate pranks but apparently struggling with basic illusion theory. Recent onset of problems, urgent need for help, faculty concern about magical inconsistencies.

It sounded less like academic trouble and more like something was going wrong with his magic itself.

And despite my better judgment, despite my carefully planned schedule and my important research deadlines, I had to admit I was curious to find out what.

After all, I'd built my entire academic reputation on solving complex magical problems. How hard could one fox shifter be?

———

BY THE TIME I made my way to the Dining Hall for lunch, my morning's research session had yielded excellent results. The aurora variance data was even more promising than I'd hoped, and I'd managed to draft the first section of my theoretical framework for the sustainability study.

It had been a productive morning. So why did I feel so... restless?

The Dining Hall hummed with its usual midday energy—hundreds of conversations creating a symphony of excitement, gossip, and caffeine-fueled stress. I collected my usual lunch (grilled aurora salmon, crystallized vegetables, and mint tea) and scanned the room for an empty table.

Most students ate in groups, clustering around the round tables that accommodated different magical species' social structures. The reindeer shifters held court near the tall windows, their antlers catching the light as they discussed what sounded like Reindeer Games strategy. A table of winter sprites near the fireplace filled the air with tinkling laughter that sounded like wind chimes. The elves maintained their elegant composure at a table draped with silver cloth, their conversation too quiet to overhear but probably involving poetry or philosophy.

And then there were the spaces between—the quiet corners and small tables where students like me ate alone.

I was settling into my usual spot by the eastern wall when a burst of laughter from the shifter section caught my attention. The sound was warm and infectious, the kind of laugh that made other people smile even if they didn't know what was funny.

Dylan Vixen.

He sat at the center of a group of fox and wolf shifters, gesturing animatedly as he told some story that had his friends hanging on every word. His rust-colored hair caught the magical lighting, and even from across the room, I could see the way his green eyes sparkled with mischief.

He looked completely at ease, surrounded by friends who clearly adored him. It was hard to imagine someone like that needing tutoring help, much less the "urgent" kind.

But as I watched, I noticed something that made me pause. When he thought no one was looking, his expression shifted— just for a moment—from confident charm to something that looked almost like worry. It was gone so quickly I might have imagined it, replaced by another easy grin as one of his friends made a joke.

Interesting.

"Staring at the popular kids, Lumina?"

I turned to find Marcus Evergreen sliding into the seat across from me, his silver hair catching the light in a way that marked him clearly as winter fae. We'd been study partners in Advanced Theoretical Magic since freshman year, drawn together by mutual academic intensity and a shared preference for quiet conversation over social dramatics.

"Observing," I corrected primly. "There's a difference."

"Uh-huh." Marcus followed my gaze to the shifter table, where Dylan was now balancing what appeared to be three spoons on his nose while his friends cheered. "Let me guess—new tutoring client?"

"How did you know?"

"Because you only get that particular expression when you're trying to solve a puzzle." He took a bite of his crystallized fruit salad. "And Dylan Vixen has been acting weird lately. Weirder than usual, I mean."

That got my attention. "Weird how?"

Marcus shrugged. "Little things. Magic not working quite right in shared classes. He tried some illusion spell during Elemental Theory last week, and it went completely sideways— turned Professor Ember's hair purple for three days."

"That doesn't sound unusual for a prankster."

"No, but the way he reacted did. Most fox shifters would laugh it off, you know? Make it part of the joke. But Dylan looked... scared. Just for a second, but still."

I filed that information away, adding it to my growing assessment of the Dylan Vixen puzzle. *Magical inconsistencies. Fear disguised as humor. Urgent need for help.*

"Have you heard any other rumors about his magic having problems?"

"A few. Nothing concrete, but..." Marcus leaned forward, lowering his voice. "My roommate's in Advanced Shifting Theory with him. Said Dylan's been having trouble with basic transformations lately. Nothing dramatic, just... off. Like his fox form isn't quite settling right."

He fiddled with his fork, not quite meeting my eyes. "Just... watch your back, okay? Guys like Dylan get away with a lot." His tone was casual. Too casual.

Very interesting. Both the information about Dylan's shifting problems and Marcus's oddly protective reaction. I filed both away for future consideration.

"Thanks, Marcus. That's... helpful context."

"Planning to fix him?"

There was something in his tone that made me look up sharply. Marcus was watching me with an expression I couldn't quite read—something hovering between concern and something else I couldn't identify.

"I'm planning to tutor him," I said carefully. "That's what tutors do."

"Right." He was quiet for a moment, then seemed to shake himself. "Just... be careful, okay? Fox shifters like Dylan Vixen are used to charming their way out of problems. Don't let him charm his way out of actually doing the work."

I almost smiled. "Marcus, I think you may be overestimating both his charm and my susceptibility to it."

But as I glanced back at the shifter table, catching another glimpse of Dylan's easy smile and the way it didn't quite reach his eyes, I wondered if I was overestimating my own immunity to whatever magnetic quality drew people into his orbit.

After all, I was already more curious about him than I'd been about any tutoring client in months.

And curiosity, in my experience, could be a dangerous thing.

Especially when it came wrapped in rust-colored hair and green eyes that held secrets behind their mischievous sparkle.

I pulled out my planner and composed a brief message: *Mr. Vixen, I can accommodate your tutoring request. Please meet me in the Library of Lights tomorrow at 4 PM. Come prepared to discuss your specific magical concerns in detail. - L. Lumina*

Professional. Direct. Appropriately formal.

As I sent the message, I caught myself hoping his "specific magical concerns" would prove as intellectually interesting as Professor Lumina seemed to think they would be.

Because, despite my better judgment, despite my carefully structured schedule and my important research deadlines, I was finding myself genuinely curious about what had shaken the confidence of NPU's most notorious fox shifter—and what kind of light he was hiding beneath all that charm.

And that curiosity felt dangerously close to something I hadn't experienced in years: genuine interest in another student as more than just an academic challenge to solve.

Focus, Lyra, I told myself firmly. *He's a tutoring client, nothing more.*

But even as I turned back to my aurora variance calculations, I couldn't quite shake the feeling that Dylan Vixen was going to be far more complicated than any magical theory I'd ever attempted to master.

CHAPTER THREE

THE FIRST SPARK

DYLAN

If there was one thing I'd learned in my nearly two years at North Pole University, it was that light magic exams were basically designed to expose every flaw in your magical foundation. Unlike illusion magic, which could be finessed with creativity and misdirection, light magic demanded precision, control, and mathematical understanding of luminous energy patterns.

In other words, everything I was terrible at.

I stared down at the exam paper in front of me, the questions seeming to blur together in a haze of technical terminology and complex magical equations. *Calculate the optimal refraction angle for sustained aurora light channeling in a temperature differential of minus forty degrees Celsius.*

Right. Because that was obviously something every fox shifter needed to know.

Around me, other students worked with varying degrees of confidence. The light magic specialists—mostly sprites and a few winter elves—moved through the problems with fluid ease, their quills scratching steadily across the parchment. Even the non-specialists seemed to be managing better than I was.

I glanced toward the front of the classroom, where Professor Lumina presided over the exam with her characteristic serene authority. Her pale hair caught the magical lighting, and her ice-blue eyes swept the room with the kind of attention that missed nothing. This was Lyra's guardian—the woman who'd raised NPU's most brilliant student.

Speaking of Lyra...

I spotted her three rows ahead and to the left, her dark hair falling in a neat curtain as she bent over her exam. Even from behind, I could see the confidence in her posture, the way her hand moved across the page without hesitation. She was probably already on the bonus questions while I was still struggling with the basics.

The appointment confirmation she'd sent yesterday had been perfectly professional: *"Mr. Vixen, I can accommodate your tutoring request. Please meet me in the Library of Lights tomorrow at 4 PM. Come prepared to discuss your specific magical concerns in detail. - L. Lumina"*

Formal. Efficient. Intimidating as hell.

I turned back to my exam, panic starting to claw at my chest. If I failed this test, it would tank my already precarious GPA. If my grades slipped any further, Coach Prancer would drop me from Reindeer Games consideration faster than I could say "academic probation."

Think, Dylan. You're supposed to be clever, right?

The solution hit me like a bolt of inspiration—or desperation, depending on how you looked at it—illusion magic. If I couldn't solve the light magic problems legitimately, maybe I could create the illusion that I had.

It was risky. Professor Lumina had a reputation for detecting magical cheating with supernatural accuracy. But what choice did I have?

I closed my eyes and reached for my magic, trying to craft a simple visual illusion that would make my blank answers appear to be filled with correct responses. Just long enough to hand in the exam and escape with my dignity intact.

The magic felt... wrong from the moment I touched it.

Instead of the smooth, controllable energy I was used to, I found something jagged and unpredictable. It was like trying to hold onto lightning with my bare hands. The harder I concentrated, the more chaotic it became.

Come on, I pleaded silently. *Just one simple illusion. That's all I need.*

I poured more energy into the spell, desperation making me reckless. The magic responded, but not the way I wanted. Instead of creating false text on my exam paper, it started to build and twist, becoming something entirely different.

Something dangerous.

The first sign of trouble was the smell—that sharp ozone scent that had been following me around lately, now strong enough to make my eyes water. The second sign was the way the magical energy around me began to shimmer and distort, like heat waves rising from summer pavement.

Oh, hell.

I tried to shut down the spell, but it was too late. The magic had taken on a life of its own, spiraling out of my control with increasing intensity. The air around my desk began to glow with an eerie green light that definitely wasn't supposed to be there.

Other students were starting to notice. I caught sight of a water sprite two desks over, staring at me with wide, concerned eyes. Behind me, someone whispered, "Is that supposed to be happening?"

Professor Lumina's attention snapped to me like a laser. Her pale eyes widened fractionally—the most emotion I'd ever seen her display—as she took in the growing magical disturbance.

"Mr. Vixen," she said in a voice that carried clearly across the suddenly quiet classroom, "please step away from your desk."

But I couldn't. The magic was flowing through me now, wild and uncontrolled, and moving felt like it might make everything worse. The green glow was spreading, reaching toward other students' desks like searching fingers.

That's when Lyra Lumina did something that changed everything.

She stood up from her desk with fluid grace, her own exam forgotten, and turned to face the magical chaos I'd accidentally unleashed. For a moment, our eyes met across the classroom, and I saw something in her pale blue gaze that I hadn't expected: not judgment or disgust, but intense, analytical curiosity.

Then she raised her hands and began to weave the most beautiful magic I'd ever seen.

Light poured from her fingers—not the harsh, chaotic green of my failing spell, but pure silver radiance that seemed to sing as it moved through the air. She shaped it with precise gestures, creating what looked like a containment web around my desk.

The moment her light magic touched mine, everything changed.

Instead of the violent clash I'd expected between order and chaos, something extraordinary happened. The silver light didn't fight my wild green energy—it embraced it, wrapping around the chaotic magic like gentle hands calming a frightened animal.

The sensation was indescribable. For just an instant, I could feel Lyra's magic intertwining with mine, her control guiding my chaos into something that wasn't destructive but... beautiful. The harsh green light softened to a warm gold, and the violent energy settled into gentle, dancing patterns that reminded me of fireflies on a summer evening.

Then the spell collapsed.

Not violently, but like a sigh of relief, the combined magic dissipating into sparkles of light that faded slowly from the air. The classroom was silent except for the soft whisper of magical energy settling back into its natural state.

I found myself standing—when had I stood up?—gripping the edge of my desk so hard my knuckles were white. My heart was hammering against my ribs, and I could taste copper in my mouth. But alive. Definitely alive.

Lyra was still standing too, her hands lowered but her eyes fixed on me with an intensity that made me feel like she could see straight through to my soul. There was a faint flush in her pale cheeks, and her breathing was slightly quick, as if the magical working had affected her as much as it had me.

"Fascinating," Professor Lumina said into the silence, her voice carrying a note of something that might have been wonder. "Miss Lumina, Mr. Vixen, please remain after class. The rest of you may continue your exams."

The classroom slowly returned to something resembling normal as other students bent back over their papers, though I caught several curious glances thrown our way. I sank back into my chair, my legs suddenly feeling like overcooked pasta.

What the hell just happened?

Not just the magical disaster—though that was definitely something I needed to figure out. But the way Lyra's magic had felt when it touched mine. The way it had known exactly what my chaotic energy needed to find balance. The way she'd looked at me afterward, like she'd seen something in the magical interaction that surprised her.

I risked another glance in her direction and found her still watching me, though she quickly turned back to her exam when our eyes met. But not before I caught something in her expression that made my chest do another one of those weird flutters.

Only this time, it didn't feel like my magic malfunctioning.

This time, it felt like something else entirely.

———

THE REMAINING forty minutes of the exam passed in a blur of awkward silence and desperate attempts to actually answer some questions. I managed to scribble down responses to maybe half the problems, though whether any of them were correct was anybody's guess.

My magic felt... different now. Not fixed, exactly, but like something had shifted. The chaotic energy was still there, still unpredictable, but there was an echo of something else. Something that reminded me of fireflies on a summer evening—gentle, warm, and impossibly beautiful.

When Professor Lumina finally called time, I watched the other students file out with a mixture of relief and dread. Whatever conversation was about to happen, it wasn't going to be pleasant.

Lyra approached the front of the classroom with her characteristic poise, her completed exam in hand. Even her handwriting looked elegant from a distance. She stood at respectful attention beside Professor Lumina's desk, but I caught her stealing glances in my direction.

I gathered my things and trudged forward, my half-finished exam feeling like evidence of criminal incompetence. If there was a magical court, I'd be convicted on the first page.

"Mr. Vixen," Professor Lumina said as I handed over my paper, "are you injured? Do you need to visit the Magical Health Center?"

"No, ma'am. I'm fine." *Physically, anyway.*

"Good." She set my exam aside without looking at it—probably for the best. "Now, would you care to explain what just occurred?"

I opened my mouth, then closed it. How exactly was I supposed to explain that I'd been trying to cheat and accidentally created a magical disaster?

"I was... having some difficulty with the exam," I said carefully. "I tried to use a simple illusion spell to... clarify my thinking. But something went wrong."

Professor Lumina's pale eyebrows rose fractionally. "Clarify your thinking. I see."

She absolutely saw right through that.

"The magic felt different," I continued, deciding honesty might be my only option. "Unstable. Like it was fighting me instead of responding to my will."

"And how long have you been experiencing these... difficulties?"

I glanced at Lyra, who was listening with obvious interest. "A few weeks, maybe? It started small, but it's been getting worse."

"Hmm." Professor Lumina made a note on a piece of parchment. "Miss Lumina, your magical intervention was quite impressive. Can you describe what you observed during the interaction?"

Lyra straightened slightly, slipping into what I was starting to recognize as her academic presentation mode. "The magical energy appeared to be in a state of chaotic oscillation, possibly due to incomplete anchoring or interference from an external source. When I applied a stabilization matrix using structured light magic, the chaotic elements responded by... syncing with the stabilization pattern."

She paused, a slight frown creasing her brow. "Which shouldn't have been possible with standard magical theory."

"Indeed." Professor Lumina looked thoughtful. "And how did the interaction feel to you, personally?"

A flush crept up Lyra's neck. "It felt... natural. Like the two magical signatures were designed to complement each other." She glanced at me quickly, then away. "Though I'm sure that's just an illusion created by the stabilization process."

Was it, though?

Because it had felt like coming home—like Lyra's magic understood mine better than I did.

"Mr. Vixen," Professor Lumina continued, "I believe it would be beneficial for you to work closely with Miss Lumina on understanding these magical irregularities. She has considerable expertise in magical theory, and given this afternoon's events, she may be uniquely qualified to help you."

"I... yes, ma'am. If she's willing."

Both of us looked at Lyra, who was staring at her hands with unusual intensity. "I've already agreed to tutor Mr. Vixen in magical theory," she said quietly. "Though perhaps we should adjust the scope of our sessions to include diagnostic work as well."

"Excellent." Professor Lumina smiled—an expression that transformed her austere features entirely. "I suggest you begin immediately. Mr. Vixen, I'm postponing your exam grade pending the results of your tutorial sessions. If Miss Lumina can help you stabilize your magical difficulties, I'll allow you to retake the examination."

Relief flooded through me so intensely that I felt lightheaded. "Thank you, Professor. Really, I—"

"Don't thank me yet," she interrupted gently. "Thank Miss Lumina. She's the one who prevented what could have been a very dangerous situation."

I turned to Lyra, who was still avoiding eye contact. Up close, I could see details I'd never noticed before: the way her dark eyelashes cast shadows on her pale cheeks, the small scar above her left eyebrow, the precise way she held herself even when she was obviously uncomfortable.

"Thank you," I said, meaning it more than I'd meant anything in weeks. "I don't know what would have happened if you hadn't stepped in."

She finally looked up, meeting my eyes for just a moment. "It was the logical thing to do. Uncontrolled magical energy can be dangerous to everyone in the vicinity."

Right. Logical. Not personal, not about me specifically. Just good sense and academic responsibility.

So why did I feel like there had been something more in the way she'd worked her magic around mine? Something that went beyond logic and responsibility into territory that neither of us was ready to name?

"I should go," Lyra said suddenly, gathering her things with brisk efficiency. "I have research to complete before our tutoring session tomorrow."

"Of course. Thank you again, Miss Lumina." Professor Lumina's expression was pleased. "I have a feeling this arrangement will be... illuminating for both of you."

As Lyra headed for the door, I caught up with her in the hallway outside the classroom.

"Lyra, wait."

She paused, turning back with a carefully neutral expression. "Yes?"

"I just wanted to say... what you did back there was incredible. I've never seen magic like that."

Something flickered in her pale eyes. "It was simply applied magical theory. Nothing more."

"Was it?" I stepped closer, drawn by something I couldn't name. "Because it felt like more. It felt like..."

"Like what?" Her voice was quiet, but there was something underneath it—curiosity, maybe, or challenge.

Like coming home. Like finding something I didn't know I'd been looking for. Like magic, the way it's supposed to feel.

But I couldn't say any of that. Not to someone I barely knew, no matter how perfectly her magic had complemented mine.

"Like maybe there's more to magical theory than I thought," I said instead.

Lyra studied my face for a long moment, and I had the unsettling feeling she was seeing more than I meant to show.

"Perhaps there is," she said finally. "I suppose we'll find out tomorrow at four."

She walked away before I could respond, her footsteps echoing in the empty hallway. I watched until she disappeared around the corner, my mind replaying the moment when her silver light had wrapped around my chaotic magic and somehow made it beautiful.

Tomorrow at four.

For the first time since my magic had started acting up, I was actually looking forward to something.

Even if that something involved spending time with NPU's most intimidating academic perfectionist discussing my magical failures in embarrassing detail.

Because after what happened today, I knew the first spark had already caught fire.

CHAPTER FOUR

ASSIGNMENT: OPPOSITES

LYRA

The Library of Lights occupied the entire third floor of the Lumina Wing, and I'd spent enough hours here to know every reading nook, every carved pillar, every subtle variation in the magical illumination that danced across the crystal shelves. It was my sanctuary—a place where knowledge lived in perfect organization and conversations happened in respectful whispers.

Which was why Dylan Vixen's arrival felt like a small earthquake.

He burst through the main doors at exactly 4:03 PM, bringing with him the scent of winter air and what I was beginning to recognize as that distinctly chaotic magical energy that seemed to follow him everywhere. His rust-colored hair was windswept, his cheeks flushed from cold, and he carried himself with the kind of barely contained energy that made me instinctively straighten in my chair.

I watched from my usual study alcove as he paused just inside the entrance, green eyes scanning the vast space until they found me. When our gazes met, something flickered across his expression—surprise, maybe, or recognition of something from yesterday's magical incident that neither of us had quite managed to name.

He approached my table with that easy stride that suggested he was comfortable anywhere, even in NPU's most intimidating academic space.

"You're punctual," I observed as he settled into the chair across from me.

"Only three minutes late. That's practically early for me." His grin was self-deprecating. "Besides, I figured you'd already started without me. Probably solved half my magical problems just by thinking about them analytically."

Despite myself, I felt my lips twitch toward a smile. "Unfortunately, magical analysis requires actual observation of the magic in question. I can't diagnose problems through theoretical speculation alone."

"Right. So, where do we start? Fair warning—my magical problems are probably more creative than anything you've encountered before."

There was humor in his voice, but underneath it, I caught something else. Worry, maybe. The kind of carefully hidden concern that came from knowing something was wrong but not understanding what.

I pulled out a leather portfolio and opened it to reveal several sheets of parchment covered with neat handwriting. "I've prepared a comprehensive assessment framework. We'll begin with basic diagnostic exercises to establish a baseline for your magical capabilities, then move through increasingly complex applications to identify where the irregularities occur."

Dylan leaned forward to peer at my notes, and I caught a whiff of that ozone scent that had been present during yesterday's incident. Interesting. The smell seemed to be connected to his unstable magic.

"This looks... thorough," he said after a moment. "And slightly terrifying."

"Magical diagnosis requires a systematic approach. We can't solve a problem we don't fully understand."

"See, that's where you and I are different. I usually just wing it and hope everything works out."

I looked up from my notes to find him watching me with an expression I couldn't quite interpret. "How has that approach been working for you recently?"

"Point taken." He ran a hand through his hair, messing it up even more. "Okay, Professor Lumina. Where do we start?"

"I'm not a professor. And we start with this."

I reached into my bag and withdrew what looked like a standard magical contract, the kind used for tutoring arrangements throughout NPU. But this one had been modified with several additional clauses that I'd spent most of the morning perfecting.

Dylan took the parchment and read aloud: "Standard tutoring agreement between Lyra Lumina, certified magical theory specialist, and Dylan Vixen, student requesting assistance." He paused, frowning. "What's this part about 'emotional regulation enforcement'?"

"A necessary addition. Given yesterday's... incident, it became clear that emotional state can significantly impact magical stability. The contract includes clauses designed to maintain productive working conditions."

"Which means?"

I gestured to the parchment. "Read clause seven."

"If either party becomes argumentative, hostile, or otherwise disruptive to the learning environment, the contract will activate a cooling-off protocol." Dylan's eyebrows rose. "The parchment will glow with increasing intensity until both parties... cool off. What exactly does 'cool off' mean?"

"Temperature reduction spell. Localized to this table area. It activates whenever we argue too intensely and doesn't deactivate until we're both calm and focused."

Dylan stared at me. "You put a spell on our tutoring contract to make us behave?"

"I enchanted it to create optimal learning conditions. There's a difference."

"Is there?"

The parchment in his hands began to emit a faint golden glow, and the temperature around our table dropped about ten degrees. I shivered and pulled my robes more tightly around myself.

"This is ridiculous," I muttered, my breath now visible in small puffs.

"Actually, it's kind of brilliant," Dylan said, genuine admiration in his voice. "Magically enforced conflict resolution. Why didn't I think of that?"

The compliment caught me off guard, and I felt heat creep up my neck despite the supernatural chill. As we both settled into focus, the glow faded and the temperature returned to normal.

"So," Dylan continued, settling back in his chair with renewed focus, "what's the first diagnostic test?"

I consulted my notes, trying to ignore the way his praise had made something warm unfurl in my chest. "Basic light manipulation. I want to observe your magical energy patterns during a simple, controlled spell."

"Light magic isn't exactly my strong suit."

"Which is precisely why we're starting with it. Your natural magical signature will be more apparent when you're working outside your comfort zone."

I gestured, and a small orb of silver light appeared floating between us. "I want you to change its color. Nothing complex—just shift it from silver to any other color you prefer."

Dylan nodded, closing his eyes briefly in concentration. I watched his face as he reached for his magic, noting the slight furrow between his brows and the way his hands tensed slightly.

The moment his magic touched the light orb, I felt it.

Not just the chaotic energy I'd observed yesterday, but something deeper. His magical signature was... fractured, somehow. Like a song being played with several instruments slightly out of tune. There was power there—considerable power—but it wasn't flowing properly.

The light orb flickered through several colors rapidly—green, blue, deep purple, gold—before settling on a warm amber shade that reminded me of autumn leaves.

"How was that?" Dylan asked, opening his eyes.

"Functional, but inefficient," I said, noting the heavy energy draw.

"Story of my life. Work harder, not smarter."

The self-deprecating humor was back, but I was beginning to recognize it as his default response to anything that made him uncomfortable. Deflection through charm.

"May I try something?" I asked.

"Sure. What did you have in mind?"

Instead of answering, I reached out and lightly touched his wrist where it rested on the table. The moment our skin made contact, I let a thin thread of my own magic extend toward his.

The effect was immediate and startling.

Dylan's chaotic magical energy responded to mine like iron filings to a magnet, organizing itself into cleaner, more coherent patterns. The fractured quality smoothed out, becoming something that felt almost... harmonious.

"Whoa," Dylan breathed, staring down at where my fingers rested against his wrist. "That feels..."

"Different," I finished, because I could feel it too. My own magic, which was normally precise and controlled, seemed to be taking on some of his spontaneous energy. The combination felt more alive somehow, more dynamic than either of our signatures alone.

I should have pulled my hand away. This was supposed to be a diagnostic session, not an exploration of whatever strange resonance existed between us.

Instead, I found myself asking, "Can you try the light spell again? While I'm maintaining contact?"

This time, when Dylan reached for his magic, the change in the light orb was smooth and effortless. The amber light shifted to deep green—his signature color—with none of the chaotic flickering from before.

"That was..." He looked up at me, and for a moment, our faces were very close across the small table. Close enough that I could see flecks of gold in his green eyes, close enough to catch the faint scent of pine and winter air that seemed to cling to him.

"Interesting," I said, though the word felt inadequate for whatever had just happened.

"Yeah. Interesting."

Neither of us moved to break the contact. My hand was still on his wrist, and I could feel his pulse—quick and strong—beneath my fingertips. There was something hypnotic about the way our magic continued to weave together, creating patterns neither of us could have achieved alone.

"So," Dylan said quietly, "any theories about what's causing my magical... irregularities?"

I forced myself to focus on the academic question, though part of my mind was still marveling at the way his magic felt against mine. "Preliminary assessment suggests your magical energy isn't properly anchored. It's as if your power is trying to flow in patterns that don't quite match your natural channels."

"Which means?"

"I'm not sure yet. It could be a developmental issue—sometimes, magical abilities evolve during late adolescence in ways that require adjustment. Or it could be external interference of some kind."

"External interference?"

"A curse, magical contamination, or even just prolonged exposure to incompatible magical fields." I finally made myself pull my hand back, immediately missing the sense of magical harmony. "We'll need more data to determine which."

Dylan flexed his fingers, staring at his hands as if seeing them for the first time. "And in the meantime?"

"We continue with diagnostic testing. And..." I hesitated, then decided honesty was the most practical approach. "It seems clear that our magical signatures have some kind of stabilizing effect on each other. We may need to incorporate that into our sessions."

"You mean more of the hand-holding thing?"

Heat flooded my cheeks. "Magical contact. For therapeutic purposes. There's nothing... personal about it."

Dylan's grin was knowing. "Of course not. Purely academic."

The contract began to glow again, and we both burst into laughter as the magical cold swept over our table.

"This is going to be an interesting semester," he said once the temperature returned to normal.

"Academically speaking," I agreed.

"Right. Academically."

But there was something in his expression that suggested we

both knew this tutoring arrangement was going to be anything but purely academic.

And despite every logical instinct telling me to maintain professional boundaries, I found myself looking forward to finding out exactly how interesting things were going to get.

———

WE SPENT the next hour working through increasingly complex diagnostic exercises. The pattern that emerged was both fascinating and concerning: Dylan's magic was undeniably powerful, but consistently unstable unless I provided magical support through physical contact.

"It's like you're some kind of magical stabilizer," Dylan said as we packed up. "Which is probably the most romantic thing anyone's ever said to you me, in a deeply nerdy way."

I shot him a sharp look, but he was grinning, clearly pleased with himself for making me blush again.

"It's an unusual phenomenon," I said primly. "I'll need to research the theoretical foundations before we can develop a proper treatment plan."

"So more sessions like this?"

"Multiple sessions. Twice weekly, at minimum, until we can identify the underlying cause of your magical instability."

"And more magical contact?"

"If necessary for diagnostic purposes, yes."

Dylan stood and shouldered his bag, but he didn't move to leave. Instead, he looked around the Library of Lights as if seeing it for the first time.

"You know, I don't think I've ever actually spent time in here before," he said. "It's... this place is like your version of a fox den, isn't it?"

Something about the unexpected comparison made me pause. "It's where I can hear myself think."

"Makes sense." He nodded, understanding flickering in his green eyes. "Somewhere safe to just... be yourself."

He understood. This charming fox shifter, who thrived on social chaos, understood why I needed this quiet sanctuary.

"I should go," he said after a moment. "But Lyra? Thanks. For yesterday and today. I know tutoring some screw-up fox shifter wasn't exactly on your academic agenda."

"You're not a screw-up," I said quietly. "Your magic is different, not broken. There's a distinction."

Something shifted in his expression—surprise, maybe, or gratitude. "Same time Thursday?"

"Thursday at four. And Dylan?"

"Yeah?"

"Try to be on time."

His grin was pure mischief. "I'll do my best. But no promises."

After he left, I sat alone in the Library of Lights, staring at the magical contract. The parchment looked perfectly innocent now, no sign of the chaos it had managed whenever we'd gotten too heated.

Magical stabilizer, Dylan had called me. The description was more accurate than he realized. Our combined magical signatures created harmony that went both ways—his chaos organized my rigid control, while my structure channeled his wild energy.

It was fascinating from a theoretical perspective.

It was also terrifying from a personal one.

Because, despite my best efforts to keep this arrangement purely academic, Dylan Vixen was going to challenge more than just my understanding of magical theory.

He was going to challenge everything I thought I knew about keeping my carefully ordered world intact.

CHAPTER FIVE

POWER DISPLAY

DYLAN

Three days after our first official tutoring session, I was starting to think Lyra Lumina might actually be some kind of magical genius.

Not that this was exactly breaking news—everyone at NPU knew she was brilliant. But there was a difference between knowing someone was academically gifted and watching them work through complex magical theory as if it were simple arithmetic.

I'd arrived at the Library of Lights precisely on time (miracle of miracles) to find her surrounded by what looked like half the magical theory section. Ancient texts lay open beside modern research journals, their pages covered with her neat annotations. Floating above the table, she'd created a three-dimensional light diagram that showed magical energy flow patterns in gorgeous, shifting detail.

"Please tell me that's not all homework," I said, sliding into the chair across from her.

Lyra looked up from a particularly dense-looking tome, and I caught a brief flash of something that might have been excitement before her usual composed expression settled back into place.

"Research. I've been investigating magical resonance phenomena since our last session." She gestured to the floating diagram, which pulsed gently as it rotated. "Traditional magical theory suggests that compatible magical signatures should complement each other, but what we experienced was more than simple compatibility."

"Meaning?"

"Meaning I think your magical instability might not be a problem at all. It might be an evolution."

I blinked. "Come again?"

Lyra's eyes lit up—literally lit up, with that inner glow that happened when she got really excited about magical theory. "Look at this."

She waved her hand, and the floating diagram shifted, showing two distinct magical signature patterns. One was orderly and precise—clearly hers. The other was chaotic and wild, with energy spikes that seemed to follow no logical pattern.

"That's mine," I said, recognizing the messy signature. "Looks about right."

"Exactly. Now watch what happens when I simulate them interacting."

The two patterns began to move toward each other in the diagram. The moment they touched, something beautiful happened. Instead of clashing or one overpowering the other, they began to weave together, creating something entirely new. The chaotic spikes smoothed into flowing curves, while the rigid precision gained dynamic movement.

"It's like they're dancing," I said, genuinely amazed.

"It's like they're completing each other," Lyra corrected, though there was a slight flush in her cheeks. "Dylan, I don't think your magic is broken. I think it's designed to work in partnership with another magical signature."

"Partnership magic?" I'd heard of it, vaguely. Mostly in old legends about ancient magical bonds. "But that's—"

"Extremely rare, yes. Which is why it's taken so long to identify." She leaned forward, her excitement making her forget her usual careful reserve. "According to Aldrich's *Theories of Complementary Magic*, partnership bonds were once common among magical families. The Selwyn texts mention entire academies built around dual-casting principles."

She gestured, and another section of the floating diagram appeared, showing what looked like architectural blueprints made of light.

"Think about it. Fox shifters are naturally social creatures. Your magic evolved for pack dynamics, for working in groups. But modern magical education focuses on individual achievement, individual mastery. What if that's exactly wrong for someone like you?"

The excitement in her voice was infectious, and I found myself leaning forward to match her intensity. "So you're saying my magic's been waiting for someone?"

The words came out more vulnerable than I'd intended, and Lyra's expression softened.

"I'm saying your magic is seeking the connection it needs to function properly. And for some reason, it's found that connection with mine."

For some reason. Right. Like there wasn't something deeper happening here, something that went beyond magical theory and academic curiosity.

"So what does that mean for fixing my problems?"

"It means we might need to reconsider what 'fixing' looks like." Lyra began shuffling through her research notes. "Instead of trying to force your magic into individual patterns, we could explore developing your partnership abilities."

"With you."

"Well, yes. Since our magical signatures appear to be naturally compatible, it would make sense to—"

"Lyra."

She stopped mid-sentence, looking up at me with those pale blue eyes that seemed to see everything.

"This isn't just about magical compatibility, is it?"

For a moment, something flickered across her face—surprise, recognition, maybe even hope. But then her walls went back up, and she was Professor Lumina's perfect academic protégé again.

"I don't know what you mean. This is a theoretical exploration of partnership magic dynamics."

"Right. Theoretical."

"Completely theoretical."

"Because there's definitely nothing personal about the way our magic feels when it touches."

"Nothing whatsoever."

"And the fact that I can't stop thinking about our last session has nothing to do with you and everything to do with academic curiosity."

Lyra went very still. "Dylan..."

"Because I've got to tell you, the way you looked when our magic connected—like you'd found something you didn't know you were looking for—that didn't feel very theoretical to me."

The temperature around our table began to drop.

We both looked down at the tutoring contract, which was starting to emit that familiar golden glow.

"Seriously?" I said. "We're going to get magically cooled off for having an honest conversation?"

"This is just a tutoring arrangement—with a few magical side effects."

The contract's glow intensified, and frost began forming on the edges of the table.

"Oh, come on," I muttered, but I was talking to the wrong magical artifact.

Because Lyra's own magic was starting to respond to her emotional state, and it was doing things I'd never seen before.

Brilliance began to emanate from her skin—not the controlled, precise magic she usually wielded, but something raw and powerful. It started as a soft silver shimmer around her hands and spread upward, making her hair gleam and her eyes blaze with inner fire.

"Lyra," I said carefully, "your magic is doing something interesting."

She looked down at her hands as if noticing the light for the first time. "I'm fine. It's just a minor flare due to emotional stress."

"That's not minor."

The light was growing brighter, spreading beyond her body to illuminate the entire alcove. Around us, conversations began to fade as other students turned to stare. I heard someone whisper, "Is that supposed to happen?" and another voice hissed, "Should we get a professor?"

"I can control it," Lyra said, but silver flames were dancing in her eyes now, and her voice carried an undertone of power that made the air itself seem to vibrate.

The tutoring contract was blazing like a sunstone now, clearly overwhelmed by whatever this magic was becoming.

"I'm sure you can. But maybe you don't have to."

I reached across the table and took her hand.

The moment our skin touched, her wild luminescence and my chaotic energy slammed together with enough force to make the air around us ring like a bell. But instead of the violent collision I'd expected, they merged into something that was part quick-silver radiance, part golden warmth, and entirely beyond anything I'd ever experienced.

The combined magic poured out from our joined hands, flowing across the table, up the walls, and into every surface of the Library of Lights. Everywhere it touched, hidden patterns began to appear. Symbols carved into the crystal shelves started to glow. Runes etched into the window frames blazed to life.

And in the wall behind Lyra's usual reading alcove, something extraordinary happened.

A section of what I'd always assumed was a solid crystal wall began to shimmer and fade, revealing a passage that definitely hadn't been there before.

The entire library fell silent.

Then chaos erupted.

"Impossible," someone breathed.

"Did they just—?"

"The hidden archive! I thought that was a myth!"

The head librarian, a stern ice elf named Magistrix Frost, came rushing over with her robes billowing behind her. "What have you done?" she demanded, though her voice carried more awe than anger. "That passage has been sealed for over two centuries!"

Students were gathering now, forming a loose circle around our table as they stared at the revealed opening. I caught fragments of whispered conversations: "Partnership magic," and "just like the old stories," and "are they bonded?"

Lyra stared at the newly revealed passage, her mouth slightly open in shock. "That's... that's not supposed to be there."

"I'm guessing it's been there all along," I said, not letting go of her hand. "Just hidden."

"But why would there be a hidden passage in the Library of Lights? And why would our magic reveal it?"

Before I could answer, Professor Lumina's voice cut through the stunned chatter.

"Because, Miss Lumina, some knowledge is meant to be discovered only by those with the proper keys."

The crowd parted as she approached, her pale robes rustling softly against the crystal floor. Her expression was serene, but I caught a glimmer of satisfaction in her ice-blue eyes.

"Professor," Lyra began, "I can explain—"

"I'm sure you can. But first, I think we should explore what you've uncovered." She gestured toward the revealed passage. "After all, it would be a shame to let such a significant magical discovery go uninvestigated."

"Everyone else, please return to your studies. Miss Lumina and Mr. Vixen will be accompanied by proper supervision."

The crowd began to disperse, though I noticed several students lingering nearby, clearly hoping to overhear whatever happened next.

Lyra looked at me, then at the passage, then back at me. "This is because of us, isn't it? Our combined magic?"

"Looks that way."

"That's... that's impossible. Hidden passages don't just respond to random magical flares."

"Maybe it wasn't random." I squeezed her hand gently, feeling the way our magic continued to pulse together in harmony. "Maybe some things are meant to be found by the right people at the right time."

"That's not how magic works."

"Isn't it?"

For a moment, Lyra just stared at me. Then, to my complete amazement, she smiled—not her careful, controlled academic smile, but something genuine and wondering and beautiful.

"I suppose," she said quietly, "we'll have to find out."

————

THE PASSAGE LED to a small chamber that felt like stepping into a forgotten dream. The air inside hummed with old magic, thick with the scent of enchanted parchment and winter pine. As we crossed the threshold, faint light bloomed from the walls as if reacting to our presence, casting golden shadows that flickered like candle flames.

The walls were covered with murals depicting what appeared to be ancient magical partnerships—pairs of figures whose magic combined to create incredible feats of power and beauty. Some showed partners calling down storms together, others healing great wounds, still others crafting artifacts that glowed with impossible radiance.

"Partnership magic," Lyra breathed, moving to examine the nearest mural. "This is all about partnership magic."

I followed her deeper into the chamber, our hands still joined, our magic still humming together in that impossibly perfect harmony. As I stared at the painted figures, a memory stirred—something I'd buried so deep I'd almost forgotten it existed.

I was seven years old, sitting in the back of Advanced Magical Theory for Young Shifters, watching other kids perform spells with effortless grace while mine sputtered and failed. Professor Blackwood had pulled my parents aside after class, his voice carefully controlled as he explained that some children simply developed more slowly than others.

"Perhaps Dylan would benefit from individual instruction,"

he'd suggested. "Group dynamics seem to... overwhelm his natural abilities."

But it hadn't been overwhelming. Looking back now, I realized it had been the opposite. I'd been trying so hard to match everyone else's solo performance that I'd never learned to let my magic reach for the connections it actually needed.

"Think this is why we found it?" I asked, shaking off the memory.

"I think," Professor Lumina said from the passage entrance, "that you two have stumbled onto something far more significant than a simple tutoring arrangement."

She moved into the chamber with us, her gaze taking in the murals with obvious recognition.

Lyra turned to face her guardian. "Did you know this was here?"

Professor Lumina's smile was enigmatic. "I suspected. The founders of North Pole University were great believers in partnership magic. They built this institution on the principle that magical knowledge grows strongest when shared between compatible minds."

She approached one of the larger murals, which showed two figures whose combined magic was creating what looked like the crystalline spires of NPU itself.

"This chamber was sealed when individual magical education became the dominant paradigm. But the founders left... contingencies. Ways for the old knowledge to reveal itself when the right students were ready."

"And you think we're ready?" I asked.

"I think," Professor Lumina said gently, "that your magic has been trying to tell you something important. Perhaps it's time you listened."

She moved closer to Lyra, and for a moment, her composed

expression flickered with something deeper. "Your parents would be proud, you know. They understood partnership magic better than most. Your mother always said the right magical bond could change the course of magical history."

Lyra went very still. "My parents?"

"Another conversation for another time, dear one. For now, you should explore what you've discovered. Learn what these walls have to teach you."

She headed back toward the passage, but paused at the threshold. "Oh, and children? This discovery will need to remain between us for now. Partnership magic is... politically complex. Best to understand what you're dealing with before word spreads."

After she left, Lyra and I stood alone in the ancient chamber, surrounded by murals celebrating magical partnerships that had spanned centuries.

"She's been planning this," Lyra said quietly.

"Seems like it."

"The tutoring arrangement, the way she encouraged me to work with you specifically..." She turned to look at me, and I could see understanding dawning in her pale eyes. "She knew we were compatible."

"Smart woman."

"Dylan, what if she's right? What if my magic has been trying to tell me something?"

I looked around at the painted figures, at the way their magic flowed together in perfect harmony, and felt something settle into place in my chest—something that had been restless and searching for longer than I cared to admit.

"Maybe mine wasn't broken at all," I said. "Maybe it had just been waiting—for you."

The words hung in the air between us, loaded with possibility and promise and the kind of truth that changed everything.

Lyra's fingers tightened around mine, and for the first time since I'd known her, she looked at me without any of her careful academic distance.

"I suppose," she said softly, "we'll have to see where this leads."

As our combined magic painted the ancient chamber in warm aureate patterns, I couldn't help but think that wherever it led, we were going to face it together.

And for the first time in my life, that felt exactly right.

CHAPTER SIX

EXTRAORDINARY WORLDS COLLIDE

LYRA

I'd never brought anyone to the Light Observatory before.

Not Marcus, despite years of study partnership. Not the handful of tutoring students who'd earned my professional respect. Certainly not the professors who occasionally requested demonstrations of my research. The Observatory was mine—my sanctuary, my workspace, my refuge from the social complexities that seemed to trip me up everywhere else on campus.

So when I heard myself saying, "Would you like to see where I do my real research?" to Dylan Vixen as we walked back from the hidden chamber, I was almost as surprised as he looked.

The words had tumbled out before I could stop them, and now, as we made our way through the quiet evening corridors of the Lumina Wing, I found myself second-guessing the impulse. What had possessed me to invite him into my most private space? The partnership magic discovery had left me feeling raw, exposed in ways I wasn't used to. Maybe that was why my usual defenses felt paper-thin.

"Your real research?" Dylan's green eyes sparked with curiosity. "As opposed to the fake research you've been doing in the library?"

"As opposed to the research I do when I'm not trying to diagnose someone else's magical difficulties," I corrected, though there was no bite in my voice. The discovery of the partnership magic chamber had left me feeling... different. More open, somehow. Like whatever barriers I usually maintained had been temporarily dissolved by the revelation that my magic wasn't meant to work alone.

I noticed the way Dylan's steps had slowed slightly, matching my pace even though his longer stride could easily outpace me. There was something considerate about the gesture that made my chest feel warm.

"I'd love to see it," Dylan said, and something in his tone made me glance at him sideways. There was genuine interest there, not just politeness. "Fair warning though—I might ask stupid questions."

"There are no stupid questions in magical research. Only incomplete observations."

"See, that's exactly the kind of thing that makes me think you're some kind of academic superhero."

Despite myself, I smiled. "Academic superhero?"

"You know—mild-mannered student by day, world-changing magical theorist by night. Probably has a cape made of crystallized starlight or something."

The image was so ridiculous that I actually laughed. "I don't own any capes."

"Shame. You'd look good in a cape."

Heat crept up my neck, and I focused on the spiral staircase that led to the Observatory's entrance. The climb gave me time to wonder what exactly I was doing. The Observatory was private—

Professor Lumina was the only other person who'd ever been inside. It was where I kept my most ambitious projects, my wildest theoretical experiments, the work that mattered most to me.

And I was about to share it with a fox shifter who'd been a complete stranger a week ago.

A fox shifter whose magic resonates with yours in ways that shouldn't be possible, I reminded myself. *A fox shifter who just helped you discover a chamber full of partnership magic that's been hidden for centuries.*

Halfway up the staircase, Dylan paused. "Lyra, you seem nervous. If this is too personal—"

"No," I said quickly, then realized how that sounded. "I mean, yes, it's personal. But I want to show you. I just... I've never shared this space with anyone before."

"Not even Marcus?"

"Especially not Marcus." The admission slipped out before I could stop it. "Marcus sees my work as competition to surpass. You see it as... something else."

"What do I see it as?"

I turned to look at him, standing one step below me on the crystalline stairs, his expression patient and curious.

"As if it matters," I said quietly. "As if what I'm trying to discover could actually change things."

Dylan's smile was soft. "Because it could. And because you matter, Lyra. What you're doing up there—" he gestured toward the Observatory entrance above us "—it's not just an academic exercise. It's important."

The simple validation made my throat tight. How long had it been since someone had said my work mattered? Not just that it was impressive or academically sound, but that it was *important*?

When we reached the Observatory's entrance, I paused with

my hand on the crystal door handle. "Dylan, before we go in—this space is... important to me. It's where I work on projects that aren't ready for academic review. Things that might seem impossible or impractical."

"You mean the good stuff."

I looked back at him, surprised by the understanding in his expression.

"Come on, Lyra. You think I don't recognize the difference between homework and passion projects? I may not be an academic genius, but I know what it looks like when someone cares about something enough to risk being wrong."

The simple observation hit deeper than it should have. How long had it been since someone recognized that my research was about more than grades or academic achievement? That it was about pushing boundaries, exploring possibilities, and asking questions that might not have comfortable answers?

"Yes," I said quietly. "The good stuff."

I opened the door and led him inside.

The Observatory at twilight was breathtaking. Aurora patterns danced across the transparent dome overhead, painting everything in shifting veils of green and violet. My research stations formed concentric circles around the central platform, each one dedicated to a different aspect of magical theory. Floating displays showed energy patterns, magical formulas hung suspended in mid-air, and delicate instruments tracked celestial influences on magical resonance.

But it was Dylan's reaction that made me see the space with new eyes.

He stopped just inside the doorway, his mouth slightly open as he took in the organized chaos of my life's work. Then, slowly, he began to move through the space with the careful attention of someone exploring a cathedral.

"Lyra," he said softly, approaching my aurora variance display, "this is incredible."

I watched him pause at each station, his green eyes taking in the complexity of instruments I'd built or modified myself. When he reached my experimental light-weaving loom, he stopped completely.

"Is this...?" He gestured to the delicate framework where I'd been attempting to physically manifest magical equations.

"A prototype for translating mathematical theory into tangible magical constructs," I said, moving to stand beside him. "It's based on the principle that if magic follows mathematical laws, those laws should be expressible in physical form."

"That's brilliant." Dylan reached toward the loom, then stopped. "May I?"

I nodded, watching as he lightly touched one of the crystalline threads. The moment his magic made contact, the entire framework lit up, equations flowing through the threads like liquid starfire.

"Oh," I breathed, staring at the display. "That's never happened before."

"Your magic's been waiting for a catalyst," Dylan said, wonder in his voice. "Look."

He was right. The loom wasn't just lighting up—it was weaving. Complex theoretical frameworks I'd been struggling with for months were practically writing themselves across the luminescent threads, guided by the interaction between his chaotic energy and my structured patterns.

"This isn't just theory," he continued, moving toward my seasonal fluctuation studies. "This is... you're trying to predict how magic itself evolves, aren't you?"

I blinked. "How did you—most people can't see the practical applications when I show them the mathematical models."

"Most people aren't trying to figure out why their own magic keeps changing in ways that don't make sense." Dylan moved closer to the display, and I noticed the way the floating formulas responded to his presence, their patterns shifting as if drawn to his chaotic energy signature. "But if magic evolves seasonally, and partnership magic works by combining complementary patterns..."

"Then magical instabilities might not be problems at all," I finished, watching with fascination as he worked through the logical connections. "They might be adaptations."

"Exactly." He turned to face me, excitement illuminating his features. "Lyra, what if fox shifter magic has been evolving toward partnership casting for generations, but we never realized it because modern magical education separated us from potential partners?"

The hypothesis was brilliant. And terrifying. Because if he was right, it meant that magical education itself might be inadvertently damaging students like Dylan—forcing them into individual casting patterns their magic wasn't designed for.

I found myself thinking of my first year at NPU, sitting alone in the common rooms while other students formed study groups and friendships that seemed to come so naturally to them. I'd told myself I preferred solitude, that I worked better alone. But what if that had been defensive? What if I'd built the Observatory not just as a workspace, but as a refuge from the loneliness I was too proud to admit?

"That would mean thousands of shifters have been struggling with 'defective' magic when they actually just needed compatible partners," I said slowly.

"Which would explain why my problems got worse this year. The magic is getting stronger, more insistent about finding its natural patterns."

I moved to one of my research stations and began pulling up files, my mind racing with possibilities. "If your hypothesis is correct, we should be able to track the progression. Map your magical development against seasonal changes, cross-reference with partnership magic principles..."

"Lyra."

I looked up from the data streams I was calling up to find Dylan watching me with an expression I couldn't quite interpret.

"What?"

"You're amazing."

The simple statement hit me like a physical blow. Not because it was unexpected—though it was—but because of the way he said it. Like he'd just discovered something wonderful and wanted to share it with the world.

"I'm just... applying logical analysis to available data."

"No, you're not." Dylan stepped closer, and I caught that familiar scent of winter air and chaotic magic that seemed to follow him everywhere. "You're seeing connections no one else would think to look for. You're asking questions that could change how we understand magic itself."

He gestured to the Observatory around us, taking in months of work, years of careful research, dreams made manifest in crystallized brilliance and mathematical poetry.

"This isn't just impressive, Lyra. This is revolutionary. And you've been doing it alone, up here, where no one could see how brilliant you really are."

My throat felt tight. "It's not... I mean, most of it is theoretical. Unproven. The academic review board would probably call it overly speculative."

"The academic review board can bite me."

The crude sentiment, delivered with such fierce protectiveness, made me laugh despite the emotional weight of the moment.

"Very scholarly," I managed.

"I'm not a scholar. I'm just someone who recognizes genius when I see it." Dylan's voice softened. "Thank you for showing me this. For trusting me with it."

Trust. Had that been what this was about? All my careful defenses, my professional boundaries, my refusal to let anyone too close—had I just demolished all of it by bringing Dylan here?

And more importantly, why did that feel like the smartest thing I'd done in years?

"I wanted you to see it," I admitted. "After the chamber, after discovering we might be magically compatible... I wanted you to understand what partnership could mean. Not just for your magic, but for magical research itself."

"Will you show me more?"

The simple request sent a thrill through me that had nothing to do with magic and everything to do with the way Dylan was looking at me—like I held answers to questions he'd been asking his whole life.

I moved to the central platform and activated the main display system. "This is what I've been working toward. A comprehensive model of how magical partnerships might enhance individual capabilities."

The Observatory filled with radiance as the display came online. Holographic figures appeared around us, demonstrating theoretical partnership casting techniques. Mathematical formulas traced themselves across the dome overhead. Energy patterns danced through the air like living things.

"Each partnership would be unique," I explained, gesturing to show how the patterns shifted and evolved. "Based on the individual magical signatures, emotional compatibility, shared intentions..."

As I spoke, I noticed Dylan moving closer to the central display. When he reached out to touch one of the floating equations, something extraordinary happened. The holographic formula solidified under his touch, becoming real, physical, and tangible.

"Did that just—?" He looked at his hand in amazement.

"Your magic is completing the theoretical framework," I said, staring at the now-solid equation floating in his palm. "Making theory into reality."

I activated another section of the display, and our own magical signatures appeared—his chaotic energy patterns interweaving with my structured precision in the familiar dance we'd witnessed in the hidden chamber.

"But some partnerships," I continued, my voice dropping to a whisper as I watched our magic flow together in perfect harmony, "would be particularly powerful."

Dylan moved to stand beside me on the platform, and immediately the holographic displays responded to his presence. The theoretical models shifted, becoming more dynamic, more alive. Our actual magical signatures began to resonate with the projected ones, creating feedback loops that made the entire Observatory pulse with warm, golden energy.

But more than that, the space itself seemed to come alive. Crystalline vines of illumination began connecting my research stations, data flowing between them in streams of pure radiance. Projects I'd been working on separately for months suddenly began integrating, combining, and evolving into something far more comprehensive than I'd ever imagined possible.

"Lyra," Dylan said quietly, "I think your magic is happy we're here together."

I looked around at the responding displays, at the way months of careful research was suddenly blooming into active demonstration, and realized he was right. For the first time since I'd begun working in the Observatory, the space felt complete.

"I think you might be right."

We stood there in comfortable silence, watching as our combined magical presence turned my theoretical research into living art. The aurora patterns overhead seemed to dance in response to our harmony, and the crystalline instruments hummed with contentment.

When Dylan reached for my hand, I didn't pull away. The moment our fingers interlaced, the Observatory's response intensified. Every project, every calculation, every dream I'd poured into this space blazed to life around us, creating a symphony of synchronized magical resonance.

"Can I ask you something?" Dylan said after a while.

"Of course."

"Why did you really bring me here?"

The question I'd been avoiding, even in my own thoughts. I considered deflecting, giving him some academically safe answer about research collaboration and magical compatibility.

Instead, I found myself telling the truth.

"Because I've been alone up here for two years, and I never realized how lonely that was until I met someone whose magic could share the space with mine." I looked down at our joined hands, watching the way our magical currents flowed together like streams converging. "I told myself I preferred solitude, that I worked better alone. But I think... I think I was just afraid."

"Afraid of what?"

"Of letting someone close enough to see how much I needed them."

Dylan turned to face me fully, and there was something in his green eyes that made my breath catch. "I like this version of you—the one who forgets to be Professor Lumina."

The reference to his teasing nickname from our early sessions made me smile. "She's still here. The careful, controlled academic. But maybe she doesn't have to be in charge all the time."

"You're not alone anymore, Lyra."

"No," I said softly, watching as our magical signatures continued their eternal dance around us, "I don't think I am."

And as the Observatory filled with the warm aureate glow of partnership magic made manifest, I finally understood what I'd been researching all along.

I hadn't just been studying magical theory.

I'd been preparing for him.

CHAPTER SEVEN

THE FOX DEN

DYLAN

The Fox Den hadn't changed since I'd been there last—which, I realized with a start, had been over a week ago. The common room in the basement of Reynard Hall still smelled like pine needles and mischief, still echoed with the particular brand of controlled chaos that came from housing two dozen fox shifters in one building. Enchanted lanterns cast dancing shadows on the walls, and someone had spelled the furniture to rearrange itself randomly every few hours, keeping everyone on their toes.

I used to love the chaos. The noise, the constant motion, the unpredictable rearranging of furniture that turned a trip across the room into an obstacle course. The scent of takeout pizza mixed with fox musk and whatever Kieran's latest enchantment experiment was producing. The sound of cards snapping against the table as Finn tried to cheat at poker using minor illusion magic, only to get caught by Jasper's superior hearing every single time.

But tonight, it all felt slightly off-kilter, like I was watching a favorite movie in a language I no longer understood.

It should have felt like coming home.

Instead, as I settled into the worn leather armchair that had always been "mine" in the corner near the fireplace, I found myself thinking about crystalline observatories and silver magic that danced with gold.

"Well, well," Finn MacTiernan said, dropping into the chair across from me with his characteristic grin. "Look what the cat dragged in. Where've you been hiding, Vixen?"

"Studying," I said, which was technically true.

"*Studying?*" Kieran Frost looked up from the card game he'd been losing at the central table. "Dylan Vixen? Actually studying? Someone check him for a fever."

The ribbing was familiar, affectionate, the kind of teasing I'd always enjoyed. But tonight it felt... different. Hollow, somehow.

"Yeah, well, turns out academic probation is a real motivator," I said, forcing my usual easy grin.

"Tell me you're not becoming one of those students who disappears into the library for weeks," said Jasper Wilde, a third-year with silver-streaked red hair who'd always been something of a mentor to the younger fox shifters. "Remember what happened to Tommy Reynard? Spent so much time studying he forgot how to have fun. Last I heard, he was working as an accountant for the Elf Tax Bureau."

A chorus of exaggerated shudders ran through the room.

"Worse than death," Finn agreed solemnly.

I laughed because it was expected, but the sound felt forced even to my own ears. A month ago, the idea of Tommy Reynard—notorious prankster turned bureaucrat—would have genuinely horrified me. Now I found myself wondering if maybe Tommy had just found something that mattered more than pranks and party tricks.

"Speaking of studying," Kieran said, abandoning his losing hand to flop onto the couch near my chair, "I heard you've been getting tutored by Princess Perfect herself."

My spine stiffened. "Princess Perfect?"

"Lyra Lumina," Jasper clarified with a smirk. "Ice queen of the light magic department. All brains, no personality. How'd you manage to get paired with her?"

Ice queen? The girl who'd trusted me with her most private space? Who smiled like starlight when her equations came to life? Who'd admitted she'd been lonely for two years because she was too afraid to let anyone close enough to see how much she needed them?

"She's not—" I started, then caught myself. Getting defensive about Lyra would only invite more teasing, and worse, it might reveal exactly how much she'd come to mean to me. "She's a good tutor. Very thorough."

"Thorough," Finn repeated with a knowing look. "Is that what we're calling it?"

"It's not like that," I said quickly.

"Right," Kieran drawled. "Because Dylan Vixen would never be interested in the challenge of melting the ice princess."

The casual dismissal of Lyra—reducing her to nothing more than a conquest to be won—made something hot and protective flare in my chest. These were my friends, guys I'd known for years, but suddenly their familiar banter felt cruel.

I knew what I was supposed to do—shrug, smirk, maybe crack a joke about magical chemistry. That's how we handled things in the Fox Den. Never too serious. Never too vulnerable. Keep it light, keep it moving, deflect with humor when things got too real.

But the thought of dismissing what Lyra and I had discovered together, of reducing it to some casual hookup or academic trans-action, made my jaw clench.

"She's not an ice princess," I said, my voice sharper than I'd intended. "She's brilliant. And dedicated. And—"

"Whoa," Jasper held up his hands, eyebrows raised. "Easy there, Romeo. We're just talking."

The room had gone quiet, all eyes on me. I realized I was grip-ping the arms of my chair hard enough that my knuckles had gone white.

"Sorry," I said, forcing myself to relax. "Long day."

But the damage was done. I could see it in their faces—curios-ity, amusement, and something that might have been concern.

"You know what you need?" Finn said after a moment, clearly trying to lighten the mood. "You need to blow off some steam. We were just planning the Great Gargoyle Caper for tomorrow night."

"The what now?"

"You know those painfully off-key singing gargoyles on Frost Hall?" Kieran's grin was wicked. "We're going to enchant them to perform a full rock opera. Complete with costume changes and pyrotechnics."

"Think Professor Blitzen will appreciate *Phantom of the Opera* performed by animated architecture?" Jasper added.

A week ago, the idea would have had me planning escape routes and alibis. Now, all I could think about was the way Lyra's magic had felt when it wrapped around mine, how it had turned chaos into harmony instead of adding to the mayhem.

"Sounds... elaborate," I said.

"Come on, Dylan." Finn leaned forward, his expression earnest. "When's the last time you did something just for the hell of it? You've been so serious lately."

"I haven't been serious—"

"You have, though," Kieran interrupted. "Ever since you started spending time with Lumina. She's changing you, man."

The words hit harder than they should have. Was Lyra changing me? And if she was, why did that feel less like a loss and more like... growth?

"Maybe that's not a bad thing," I said quietly.

The silence that followed was deafening.

"Okay," Jasper said slowly, "who are you and what have you done with Dylan Vixen?"

"I'm still me," I protested, but even as I said it, I wondered if it was true. The Dylan who'd arrived at NPU this semester wouldn't have spent evening after evening in the Library of Lights, wouldn't have found mathematical equations beautiful, wouldn't have felt his heart race at the sight of silver magic dancing through crystalline air.

"Are you?" Finn asked, and there was something almost sad in his voice. "Because the Dylan I know wouldn't choose home-work over hanging out with his friends. Wouldn't defend some stuck-up light mage who probably thinks we're all beneath her notice."

"She doesn't think that," I said, more heat creeping into my voice. "She's not stuck-up. She's just... careful. Reserved. There's a difference."

"Listen to yourself," Kieran said, shaking his head. "You sound like you're half in love with her."

The words hung in the air like a challenge. Around the room, I could feel the attention of every fox shifter, waiting for my response. Waiting for me to laugh it off, to make a joke, to deflect with humor the way I always did.

The silence stretched. Someone's enchanted couch shifted nervously, rearranging itself from a loveseat into a recliner. Cards scattered as Finn's illusion magic flickered and died. Even the floating lanterns seemed to dim, as if the room itself was holding its breath.

I looked around at faces I'd known since freshman orientation. Kieran, who'd helped me figure out the charm work for my first successful prank. Finn, who'd stayed up all night teaching me advanced poker when I was homesick and desperate for distraction. Jasper, who'd been like an older brother, always ready with advice or a listening ear when pack dynamics got complicated.

These guys had been my anchor when I'd felt lost in NPU's social maze. Their approval still mattered to me, maybe more than I wanted to admit.

Instead, I kept seeing the look in Lyra's eyes when she'd trusted me with her Observatory, when she'd admitted she'd been alone for two years. I remembered the moment when our magic had connected, when I'd felt less alone than I had in years.

"Maybe I am," I said quietly.

The room erupted.

"Holy shit, Dylan!" That was Tommy Blackfire, a freshman who'd been quietly hero-worshipping me since orientation.

"Are you serious right now?" Kieran's voice cracked like he was fifteen again.

"This is a disaster!" Finn threw his cards in the air, where they hung suspended by residual magic for a moment before fluttering down like confused butterflies.

"She's going to ruin him," someone muttered from the back of the room.

"Fox shifters don't do commitment, Dylan," another voice added. "It's not in our nature."

But Jasper just sat there, studying me with those sharp amber eyes that missed nothing.

"Guys, guys!" He raised his voice over the commotion. "Let's all calm down."

But I was done being calm. I was done pretending that what was happening between Lyra and me was just tutoring, just magical compatibility, just academic collaboration.

"You want to know the truth?" I stood up, facing my friends—my pack—with something that felt dangerously close to defiance. "Lyra Lumina is the most remarkable person I've ever met. She sees magic in ways that could revolutionize how we understand everything about our world. She's kind, and brilliant, and she makes me want to be better than I am."

"Dylan—" Finn started.

"No, let me finish." I looked around the room, taking in the faces of guys who'd been my brothers for two years. "You want to call her stuck-up? Fine. But she's earned the right to be proud of what she's accomplished. You want to call her an ice princess? You're wrong. She's not cold—she's careful. And maybe if we weren't so busy making jokes about everything, we'd understand the difference."

"Okay," Kieran said, holding up his hands. "Point taken. But Dylan, fox shifters don't do serious relationships. We're not built for it. We're tricksters, chaos-bringers. That's our nature."

"Says who?"

"Says... tradition? History? Basic shifter psychology?"

"What if tradition is wrong?" I challenged. "What if we've been limiting ourselves because it's easier than admitting we want more?"

I thought about the partnership magic chamber, about the murals showing magical bonds that had lasted centuries. About the way Lyra's structured magic had given my chaos purpose, direction, and meaning.

"What if some of us are meant for something deeper than pranks and one-night stands?"

The silence that followed felt heavy, loaded with things none of us quite knew how to say.

Finally, Jasper spoke. "You really care about her."

It wasn't a question.

"Yeah," I said. "I really do."

"And you think she cares about you too?"

I thought about the way Lyra had looked at me in the Observatory, the trust in her eyes when she'd shown me her most precious work. The way she'd admitted she'd been lonely, the way her hand had felt in mine when our magic danced together.

"I think... maybe she does. Or could."

"Well," Finn said after a long moment, "this is going to be interesting."

"What do you mean?"

"I mean," Kieran said with something that might have been the beginning of a grin, "if you're serious about this—really serious—then we've got your back. But Dylan?"

"Yeah?"

"If she breaks your heart, we're going to have to prank her into next semester. It's nothing personal. It's just pack law."

Despite everything, I found myself laughing. "I'll be sure to let her know."

"Good," Jasper said firmly. "Now, since you're apparently growing up on us, want to tell us about this magical compatibility thing? Because some of the stories floating around campus are pretty wild."

So I told them. Not everything—the Observatory felt too private to share, and I wasn't about to betray Lyra's trust—but I told them about the partnership magic, about the way our magical signatures seemed designed to work together, about the possibility that fox shifter magic had been evolving toward collaboration for generations.

"Wait, wait," Tommy interrupted, leaning forward with wide eyes. "You're saying our magic is supposed to work with other people's magic? Like, permanently?"

"Not permanently," I clarified. "More like... it functions better in partnership. Like it's been designed for collaboration."

"Sounds suspiciously like soulbond propaganda to me," Kieran said, though his skepticism sounded forced.

"Can you choose your partner?" Finn asked. "Or does the magic just... pick for you?"

"I don't know," I admitted. "We're still figuring it out. But based on what we've discovered, it seems like compatibility is both magical and emotional. The magic creates the potential, but you have to choose to explore it."

"And you've chosen," Jasper said. It wasn't a question.

"Yeah. I have."

By the time I finished explaining what I understood about partnership magic theory, the Fox Den had gone quiet in a way I'd never experienced before. Not the usual comfortable silence of guys who'd run out of things to say, but the heavy quiet that came with processing something that challenged everything you thought you knew about yourself.

"Partnership magic," Finn said slowly. "Like, real partnership magic? The kind from the old stories?"

"Looks like it."

"Dylan," Kieran said, and his voice was unusually serious, "do you have any idea how rare that is? How important?"

"I'm starting to."

Jasper leaned back in his chair, a thoughtful expression on his face. "You know, my grandmother used to tell stories about her great-great-grandmother. Said she was bonded to a winter sprite, and together they could call down blizzards that would last for weeks. Family always said it was just a legend."

"My great-uncle claimed he could speak to trees when he worked with his wood elf partner," Tommy added quietly. "Dad always laughed it off, said Uncle Marcus was just a romantic."

"What if they weren't just romantics?" I asked. "What if they were the last generation to understand something we've forgotten?"

"Maybe not." Jasper looked at me with something like respect. "If this is real, Dylan—if you've found an actual magical partner —then you're not just changing. You're evolving. And that's... that's pretty amazing."

But not everyone looked convinced. I could see doubt lingering in some faces, concern in others. Kieran was fidgeting with his cards, not quite meeting my eyes.

"What happens if it doesn't work out?" he asked finally. "If she decides she's too good for you, or if the magic fades, or if the professors decide partnership magic is too dangerous to study?"

The question hit harder than I wanted to admit. Because those were all possibilities I'd been trying not to think about.

For a second, the fear twisted in my gut. What if it did fade? What if she changed her mind once she really understood what being with a fox shifter meant? What if I was just a convenient research subject after all?

"I don't know," I said honestly. "But I know that not exploring it—not giving this a chance—would be worse than any of those outcomes."

"It is," I agreed, feeling some of the tension ease from my shoulders. "It really is."

"So," Finn said with a grin that was equal parts mischief and genuine curiosity, "when do we get to meet her? Properly, I mean?"

The idea of introducing Lyra to the Fox Den—of watching her

navigate the controlled chaos of fox shifter social dynamics—was both terrifying and oddly appealing.

"Let me ask her," I said. "She's not exactly... socially adventurous."

"We'll be good," Kieran promised. "Relatively good. Fox shifter good."

"That's what I'm afraid of."

But as the conversation shifted to other topics and the familiar warmth of pack friendship settled around me again, I found myself thinking that maybe it wouldn't be such a bad thing. Maybe it was time for my two worlds to meet.

After all, if Lyra and I were really partners—magically, academically, and maybe something more—then she was going to have to understand all of me eventually.

Even the chaotic, mischievous, utterly fox shifter parts.

She'd probably hate the prank planning sessions. She'd definitely dissect our enchantments and correct our spell forms with terrifying precision. But maybe, just maybe, she'd also laugh at our ridiculous schemes. Maybe she'd let herself be pulled into the chaos for a little while, let her guard down enough to see why this pack of troublemakers had become my family.

I wasn't sure if she'd survive ten minutes in here—or if she'd surprise us all.

And maybe she'd realize that even fox shifters could evolve beyond their reputations when they found something—someone —worth changing for.

The question was: would she want to?

CHAPTER EIGHT

THE TUTOR STRIKES BACK

LYRA

There had been a message from Professor Lumina earlier today—a brief reminder that my research deliverables were due soon, along with a subtle suggestion that I focus on "proven theoretical frameworks rather than experimental applications that might prove... unpredictable." The timing felt pointed, though Professor Lumina rarely said anything without multiple layers of meaning.

I'd been trying not to think about what "unpredictable" might mean in the context of my partnership magic research with Dylan.

The equations weren't balancing.

I stared at the floating mathematical formulas in my Observatory, their usually stable patterns flickering with an irregularity that made my eye twitch. The aurora variance calculations that had been perfectly aligned yesterday now drifted across their display like confused butterflies, refusing to maintain their proper formation.

It was deeply unsettling. My magic never behaved unpredictably. Order, precision, and a systematic approach were the foundational principles of everything I did. Yet here I was, three days after Dylan's last visit, and every spell I attempted carried the faintest echo of chaos.

His chaos.

I dismissed the displays with a sharp gesture, but even that felt different—less controlled, more impulsive than my usual measured movements. The mathematical constructs dissolved into sparkles of silver and gold that reminded me far too much of the way our magic had looked when it danced together.

This was becoming a problem.

A logical person would analyze the situation objectively. The magical resonance Dylan and I had discovered was clearly creating persistent effects in my spellwork. The solution would be to limit our contact to structured tutoring sessions, maintain professional boundaries, and avoid any activities that might intensify the magical bond.

Unfortunately, logic was proving remarkably inadequate when it came to Dylan Vixen.

I found myself thinking about him at odd moments—wondering what he was doing, whether his magic was experiencing similar disruptions, if he was thinking about me too. Yesterday, I caught myself walking past Frost Hall just to hear the gargoyles practicing what sounded suspiciously like show tunes. The magical signature woven through their enchantment had felt familiar, warm, tinged with the particular brand of mischievous energy that seemed to follow Dylan everywhere.

Had he been thinking of me when he cast that spell?

The thought made something flutter in my chest that had nothing to do with magical resonance and everything to do with the way he'd looked at me in the Observatory. Like I was something precious. Something worth protecting.

Focus, Lyra, I told myself firmly. *You have work to do.*

But as I attempted to restart my aurora variance study, I found my attention drifting to the central platform where Dylan had stood three nights ago. Where our magic had responded to each other with such perfect harmony that my carefully controlled research had transformed into something alive, dynamic, and beautiful.

There were no variables in this equation that accounted for longing.

The quiet that had once been my sanctuary now felt oppressive. I used to love the solitude of the Observatory—the way silence allowed me to hear my own thoughts, to focus completely on magical theory without social distractions. But over the past week, I'd begun to notice the difference between chosen solitude and unwanted isolation. The Observatory felt empty when Dylan wasn't here to fill it with his laughter, his questions, his chaos that somehow made my ordered world more alive.

I'd spent two years telling myself I preferred working alone. Now I was beginning to suspect I'd simply been afraid of discovering how much better everything was when shared with the right person.

A soft chime from my enchanted planner interrupted my brooding. New message. I gestured to open it, expecting another tutoring request or perhaps a note from Professor Lumina about my research progress.

Instead, Dylan's name appeared in flowing script above a brief message: *Lyra—free for an extra session tonight? I think I figured something out about the partnership magic theory. Observatory at 8? —D*

The flutter in my chest intensified. An extra session. He wanted to see me outside our scheduled appointments, wanted to share discoveries about the magic that connected us. The practical part of my mind noted that additional research sessions would advance our understanding of the phenomenon. The professional part reminded me that a thorough investigation required multiple data points.

The part of me that had been replaying his smile for three days simply said *yes* before I could overthink it.

I sent back a brief confirmation, then immediately began second-guessing myself. What if this wasn't about research at all? What if he'd realized, as I was beginning to, that what was happening between us went far beyond magical compatibility? What if he wanted to talk about the way our hands had fit together, or the way our magic had responded to emotional connection as much as intentional spellwork?

What if he wanted to explore territory that had no place in a tutoring arrangement?

The thought should have terrified me. Should have sent me rushing to compose a formal, professional response that redirected our focus to academic objectives. Instead, it made me check my appearance in the Observatory's mirrored surfaces and wonder if the simple blue robes I wore to research sessions made me look too much like Professor Lumina's dutiful protégé and not enough like... well, like myself.

Whoever that was.

———

BY EIGHT O'CLOCK, I'd managed to organize my research materials into what I hoped looked like casual academic preparation rather than nervous busy work. The Observatory's lighting was set to its most flattering setting—not that I was trying to impress anyone, simply creating optimal working conditions for detailed magical analysis.

Dylan arrived precisely on time, which was becoming a pattern that both surprised and pleased me. But something was different about him tonight. There was an energy in his movements, a confidence in his posture that hadn't been there during our previous sessions. He looked... settled. Like he'd resolved something important. Not in the way he dressed or spoke, but in the certainty behind his eyes. As if he'd made a decision and meant to keep it.

The change was subtle but unmistakable, and it made something flutter nervously in my stomach.

"Hey," he said, his green eyes bright with what looked like excitement. "Thanks for agreeing to meet tonight. I know it's outside our regular schedule."

"Academic research doesn't follow a schedule," I replied, then realized how formal that sounded. "I mean, I wanted to hear about this discovery of yours."

Dylan's smile was warm, genuine, and did absolutely nothing to help my efforts at maintaining professional composure. "It's more of a hypothesis than a discovery. But I think it might explain why our magic works so well together."

He moved to the central platform with the easy confidence that had developed over our sessions, no longer hesitant about touching my equipment or activating displays. Watching him navigate my workspace with such familiarity made something possessive and pleased purr in my chest.

"Show me," I said, joining him on the platform.

Dylan activated the partnership magic display we'd used during his first Observatory visit, but instead of simply observing the theoretical models, he began manipulating them directly. His magic flowed into the holographic constructs, making them more dynamic, more responsive.

"Look at this," he said, gesturing to where our magical signatures were represented in flowing patterns of light. "Every time we work together, the resonance gets stronger. Not just more intense—more sophisticated. Like the magic is learning."

I leaned closer to examine the display, immediately noticing what he meant. The interaction patterns between our magical signatures had evolved since our first session, developing new harmonics and connection points that hadn't existed before.

"Adaptive resonance," I breathed. "The magical bond is developing its own complexity based on repeated exposure."

"Exactly. Which means..." Dylan turned to face me, and I realized we were standing very close on the small platform. Close enough that I could see flecks of amber in his green eyes, could catch the scent of winter air, and something distinctly him that made my pulse quicken.

"Which means what?" I prompted, though my voice came out softer than intended.

"Which means this isn't just magical compatibility. It's a magical evolution. Our magic is becoming something new, something that didn't exist before we found each other."

The implications hit me like a thunderbolt. If Dylan was right, we weren't just experiencing a rare phenomenon—we were participating in the active creation of a new form of magical partnership. The research possibilities alone were staggering.

But more than that, it meant our connection was unique. Singular. Something that belonged only to us.

"Dylan," I said quietly, "do you understand what this means?"

"That we're making magical history?" His grin was boyish, excited. "That whatever this is between us, it's never happened before?"

Between us. The casual acknowledgment that there was an "us" made my heart skip entirely.

"It means," I said carefully, "that we're going to have to be very cautious about how we proceed. Magical evolution is unpredictable. There could be risks we haven't considered."

"Or," Dylan said, stepping slightly closer, "there could be possibilities we haven't imagined."

His hand moved as if to touch mine, then hesitated. The moment stretched between us, loaded with potential and uncertainty. I could feel his magic reaching toward mine, that familiar warm chaos seeking the structure I provided.

"Lyra," he said, his voice lower now, more serious, "can I ask you something?"

"Of course."

"Are you afraid of what's happening between us?"

The question cut straight to the heart of everything I'd been trying not to examine too closely. Was I afraid? Of the magic, of the research implications, of the way my carefully controlled world was becoming something I barely recognized?

Or was I afraid of admitting how much I wanted all of it?

"Yes," I said honestly. "I'm terrified."

"Of the magic?"

"Of everything." The admission came out in a rush. "Of the magic, of the way I feel when you're here, of what it means that I don't want our sessions to end. Of the fact that I arranged my entire schedule around our appointments and told myself it was just academic dedication."

Dylan's expression softened. "Lyra..."

"I'm supposed to be logical," I continued, the words tumbling out now that I'd started. "Systematic. I make plans and follow them. I don't get distracted by... by..."

"By what?"

"By wanting things I haven't accounted for in my life plan."

We were standing so close now that our magical auras were beginning to overlap, creating that familiar harmony that made everything else fade into background noise. Dylan's hand finally completed its journey, fingers intertwining with mine.

The moment our skin touched, my Observatory came alive around us. Not with the controlled, purposeful magic of research demonstrations, but with something spontaneous and joyful. Crystalline wind chimes materialized in the air, ringing out a melody I'd never heard but somehow knew. Aurora patterns painted themselves across every surface in flowing ribbons of silver and gold.

And I realized, with startling clarity, that this was what my magic looked like when it was happy.

"Your life plan," Dylan said gently, his thumb tracing patterns on the back of my hand, "does it have room for evolution?"

I looked around at the transformed Observatory, at the magical beauty we'd created simply by being honest with each other, and felt something that had been wound tight in my chest begin to relax.

"I'm beginning to think," I said quietly, "that the best discoveries happen when you're willing to deviate from the plan."

Dylan's smile was radiant. "I was hoping you'd say that."

"Why?"

"Because I have a confession to make." His free hand reached up to tuck a strand of hair behind my ear, the gentle touch sending shivers through my whole body. "I didn't ask for this session to discuss partnership magic theory."

My breath caught. "You didn't?"

"I mean, I do want to discuss it. But mostly, I just wanted an excuse to see you. To spend time with you when we weren't focused on fixing my magical problems or analyzing theoretical frameworks." His green eyes were serious now, vulnerable in a way that made my heart ache. "I wanted to see if you might want that too."

The admission hung between us like a bridge—one I could cross or retreat from, depending on how brave I was willing to be.

I thought about Professor Lumina's expectations, about my research timeline, about the carefully structured life I'd built around academic achievement and emotional distance. Then I thought about the way Dylan's magic felt like coming home, about the joy in my Observatory when he was here to share it, about the fact that loneliness was a variable I'd never properly accounted for in any of my equations.

"I do want that," I said, the words feeling like stepping off a cliff and discovering I could fly. "I want that very much."

Dylan's answering smile was bright enough to power the entire Observatory.

"Good," he said, bringing our joined hands up to rest against his chest, right over his heart. "Because I have some ideas about how we might spend our non-academic time together."

A quiet warning stirred at the back of my mind—Professor Lumina's reminder to focus on "proven frameworks." This wasn't that. Whatever Dylan and I were discovering, it wasn't sanctioned, safe, or expected. And I wasn't sure I wanted it to be.

"Such as?"

"Well," his grin turned mischievous, "have you ever been to a fox shifter bonfire? Because the guys are really curious about meeting you, and I thought maybe—if you're feeling adventurous—you might like to see what the Fox Den is actually about."

The idea of meeting Dylan's friends, of stepping into his world the way he'd stepped into mine, was both thrilling and terrifying. But looking into his hopeful, excited face, I found I wanted to be brave enough to try.

"I suppose," I said, trying for academic detachment and failing completely when my voice came out warm and eager, "that would constitute valuable anthropological research."

"Anthropological research," Dylan repeated, laughing. "Is that what we're calling it?"

"Would you prefer 'cultural exchange'?"

"I'd prefer calling it what it is," he said, his expression growing tender. "You being willing to trust me with introducing you to my family."

Family. The word settled into my chest like a missing piece clicking into place. Because that's what the fox shifters were to Dylan, wasn't it? His chosen family, his pack, the people who'd supported him long before I'd entered his life.

Family, to me, had always meant distance, expectation, and obligation. But Dylan's version looked like laughter, chaos, and unwavering loyalty. And maybe—for the first time—I wondered what it might feel like to be chosen, not expected.

I hesitated. Not because I didn't want to say yes—but because saying yes meant letting him see just how much I wanted to belong.

And he wanted me to meet them.

"When?" I asked.

The question opened a floodgate of anxieties I hadn't antici-pated. What did one wear to a fox shifter bonfire? Should I prepare conversation topics, or would that seem awkward and overly formal? I was already planning three different polite excuses I could use if the evening went disastrously wrong, while simultaneously hoping I wouldn't need any of them.

The image of Dylan in his element—surrounded by friends who clearly adored him, animated and relaxed in a way I'd only glimpsed—made me curious despite my nerves. What would it be like to see him through their eyes? To understand the world that had shaped him before our paths crossed?

Maybe I wanted to know if I could belong in that world, even temporarily.

"Tomorrow night, if you're free. Fair warning—they're loud, chaotic, and they'll probably try to teach you poker using minor illusion magic."

"I'll bring my textbook on statistical probability."

Dylan's laughter filled the Observatory, mixing with the crystal chimes that were still ringing their mysterious melody. "Lyra Lumina, I think you're going to fit in better than you know."

As our magic continued to paint aurora patterns across the dome overhead, I found myself thinking that maybe deviating from the plan wasn't such a frightening prospect after all.

Especially if it meant more evenings like this, more discoveries that had nothing to do with academic achievement and everything to do with the way Dylan looked at me like I was the most fascinating puzzle he'd ever encountered.

A puzzle he was genuinely excited to solve.

CHAPTER NINE
FOUND FAMILY PARALLEL

LYRA

I changed my outfit three times before settling on what I hoped struck the right balance between approachable and appropriately dressed for an outdoor gathering. The dark green sweater felt less formal than my usual robes, but not so casual as to suggest I was trying too hard to fit in. Which I absolutely was not doing. This was purely anthropological research into fox shifter social dynamics.

The lie felt transparent even to myself.

Standing outside Reynard Hall at precisely seven-thirty, I could hear the sounds of the Fox Den gathering before I could see it. Laughter echoed from behind the building, punctuated by what sounded like someone telling an elaborate story to an appreciative audience. The scent of woodsmoke and roasting marshmallows drifted on the evening air, mixed with the distinctive magical energy that seemed to permeate any space where fox shifters congregated.

It smelled like controlled chaos. It smelled like Dylan.

My hands were trembling slightly as I followed the stone path around the building, and I forced myself to stop and breathe. These were Dylan's friends—his family, he'd called them. The people who'd known him long before I'd entered his life, who'd watched him struggle with his magic, who'd supported him through whatever challenges had brought him to NPU.

The people whose approval might determine whether I truly belonged in his world.

"Lyra!"

Dylan's voice cut through my spiraling anxiety, warm and delighted. He appeared from around a cluster of pine trees, his face lit up with genuine happiness at seeing me. The relief that flooded through me was embarrassingly intense.

"You came," he said, reaching me in a few quick strides.

"I said I would."

"I know, but..." He paused, studying my face with those perceptive green eyes. "Are you nervous?"

There was no point in lying. "Terrified."

Dylan's expression softened. "Hey. It's just the guys. They're going to love you."

"Are they?" The question came out smaller than I'd intended. "Dylan, I'm not exactly known for my social skills. What if I say something wrong, or they think I'm too formal, or—"

"Lyra." Dylan stepped closer, his hands coming up to frame my face gently. "You're brilliant, kind, and funny when you let yourself be. Anyone who doesn't see that is an idiot."

"But what if—"

"What if they see exactly what I see when I look at you?" Dylan's thumbs traced soft patterns across my cheekbones. "Someone extraordinary who's been hiding behind academic perfection because she's forgotten how amazing she is just as herself?"

The words hit deeper than they should have. How long had it been since someone had seen me as more than Professor Lumina's protégé or the campus tutoring service? How long since anyone had cared about Lyra rather than what Lyra could do for them?

"Okay," I said quietly. "Let's go meet your family."

Dylan's smile was radiant. "That's my girl."

My girl. The casual possessiveness in his voice made something warm unfurl in my chest.

He took my hand, fingers intertwining with mine, and led me toward the sounds of the gathering. "Fair warning—they're probably going to ask you about partnership magic theory. And try to teach you poker. And potentially convince you to help with whatever elaborate prank they're planning for next week."

"I'll try to restrain myself from correcting their magical technique."

"Please don't. Kieran's been getting way too cocky about his illusion work."

The Fox Den gathering was being held in a small clearing behind Reynard Hall, where someone had built a proper bonfire surrounded by an eclectic collection of logs, camp chairs, and what appeared to be several pieces of furniture that had been spelled to rearrange themselves into seating as needed. String lights hung between the trees, casting everything in warm, golden illumination that made the whole scene look like something from a fairy tale.

About fifteen fox shifters were scattered around the fire, some roasting marshmallows, others engaged in what looked like an intense debate about magical theory. A card game was happening on a floating table that kept shifting height to accommodate players of different sizes. Someone had brought a guitar and was playing soft background music that mixed beautifully with the crackling of the fire.

It looked cozy. Welcoming. Like the kind of gathering I'd always observed from a distance but never thought I'd be invited to join.

"Everyone," Dylan called out, his voice carrying easily across the clearing. "I'd like you to meet Lyra."

The effect was immediate and slightly overwhelming. Conversations paused, heads turned in our direction, and suddenly I was the focus of more friendly attention than I'd experienced in years. But instead of the judgment or dismissal I'd half-expected, I saw genuine curiosity and what looked like a cautious welcome.

"So you're the one who's been keeping Dylan busy," said a silver-haired fox shifter who rose from one of the camp chairs. He was older than the others, with the kind of easy authority that suggested leadership. "I'm Jasper Wilde, unofficial den mother of this chaotic bunch."

"Lyra Lumina," I replied, accepting his offered handshake. "Thank you for including me."

"Dylan's told us quite a bit about you," Jasper continued with a knowing smile. "Though I suspect he's left out some of the more interesting details."

"Jasper," Dylan warned, but there was affection in his voice.

"What? I'm just saying, it's not every day someone manages to get Dylan to voluntarily spend time in the library."

A red-haired fox shifter with mischievous eyes bounded over. "I'm Finn MacTiernan. Dylan says you're some kind of magical genius. Is it true you can make equations solid?"

"It's a theoretical application of—" I began, then caught myself. This wasn't a lecture hall. "Yes. Under certain conditions."

"That's amazing," Finn said with genuine enthusiasm. "Could you show us sometime? I've been working on a prank that would benefit from some solid mathematical support."

Despite myself, I found myself smiling. "What kind of prank?"

"Well, if you could make Professor Blitzen's grade calculations temporarily solid, we could rearrange them into more... aesthetically pleasing patterns."

"That would be academic fraud," I pointed out.

"Only if we changed the actual grades. We're just talking about creative presentation."

The casual way Finn discussed magical ethics—not dismissing them, but finding creative ways to work within the boundaries—was oddly charming. This wasn't the irresponsible chaos I'd expected from Dylan's descriptions. It was structured mischief, carefully planned to avoid real harm.

"Finn, leave her alone," called another voice. A fox shifter with distinctive white streaks in his dark hair approached, looking slightly exasperated. "I'm Kieran Frost. Someone has to keep these idiots from accidentally exposing our magical signatures to half the faculty."

"Kieran's our voice of reason," Dylan explained. "Such as it is."

"Hey," Kieran protested. "I successfully talked them out of enchanting the entire dining hall to play Wagner during breakfast."

"Only because you wanted to save it for the winter formal," Finn pointed out.

As the good-natured bickering continued around me, I found myself relaxing in ways I hadn't expected. The conversation flowed easily, jumping from magical theory to campus gossip to elaborate speculation about professors' personal lives. No one seemed to expect me to prove my worth or demonstrate my academic credentials. They simply... included me.

"Lyra," Jasper said during a lull in the conversation, "Dylan mentioned you've been researching partnership magic. That's fascinating work—historically significant, too."

"You know about partnership magic?" I asked, surprised.

"My grandmother used to tell stories. Said it used to be more common, before individual magical education became the standard." Jasper's expression grew thoughtful. "She always claimed the old ways produced stronger magic, more stable spell-work."

"The old texts support that theory," I said, finding myself drawn into academic discussion despite the casual setting. "Partnership magic appears to create compound effects that exceed the sum of individual abilities."

"Is that what's happening with you and Dylan?" Kieran asked bluntly.

I felt heat creep up my neck. "We're still gathering data—"

"Oh, come on," Finn interrupted with a grin. "The whole campus knows something magical happened in the Library of Lights last week. Hidden passages don't just reveal themselves for random tutoring sessions."

"How did you—" I began, then stopped. Of course word had spread. NPU's rumor network was more efficient than most formal communication systems.

"So it's true?" A younger fox shifter I hadn't met yet leaned forward eagerly. "You really found ancient partnership magic stuff?"

"We discovered a chamber that appears to have been sealed since the university's founding," I said carefully. "It contains historical information about magical partnerships."

"That's so cool," the younger shifter breathed. "Do you think other people could learn partnership magic? Or is it just certain combinations?"

The question was exactly the one that had been keeping me awake at night. "I don't know yet. The research is still in preliminary stages."

"But you and Dylan have natural compatibility," Jasper

observed. "That much is obvious from watching you two together."

I glanced at Dylan, who was sitting close enough that our knees were almost touching. He caught my look and smiled, the kind of warm, private expression that made my pulse skip.

"It seems that way," I admitted.

"Well," Kieran said with surprising seriousness, "if partnership magic is real—if it's something that can be learned or developed—that could change everything about how we understand magical education."

"It could," I agreed. "Which is why we're being careful about how we proceed."

"Smart," Jasper nodded approvingly. "The administration tends to be... resistant to changes in magical curriculum."

Something in his tone suggested he spoke from experience.

"Speaking of administration," Finn said with a wicked grin, "has anyone told Lyra about the Great Gargoyle Opera?"

"Don't," Dylan warned.

"What's the Great Gargoyle Opera?" I asked, curiosity overriding caution.

"It's nothing," Dylan said quickly.

"It's brilliant," Kieran countered. "We've been working on a spell that would get the Frost Hall gargoyles to perform a full rock opera version of Phantom of the Opera. Complete with costume changes and pyrotechnics."

I stared at them. "You want to turn architectural elements into theatrical performers?"

"Not just any architectural elements," Finn said proudly. "Magically animated architectural elements with a documented history of responding to creative enchantments."

"The spell-work alone would be incredibly complex," I said slowly. "You'd need to coordinate individual animation charms with synchronized audio casting, plus whatever illusion magic you're using for the costumes..."

"Exactly!" Kieran's eyes lit up. "We've been stuck on the synchronization problem for weeks."

"And the pyrotechnics would require careful integration with the stone animation to avoid magical feedback," I continued, my mind automatically working through the theoretical challenges.

"Now you're getting it," Finn said with satisfaction.

I realized, with some surprise, that I was. The magical complexity of their prank was genuinely impressive, requiring the kind of multi-layered spellwork that most students wouldn't attempt until advanced courses.

"How were you planning to handle the audio synchronization?" I asked.

"We weren't sure," Dylan admitted. "We've been arguing about whether to use individual voice projection charms for each gargoyle or try to create a master enchantment that could coordinate everything."

"Master enchantment would be more efficient," I said thoughtfully. "But you'd need a way to account for the individual magical signatures of each gargoyle. They've been absorbing ambient magic for decades—they probably each have slightly different resonance patterns by now."

The fox shifters exchanged glances.

"Could you help us figure it out?" Kieran asked hopefully.

I looked around the circle of expectant faces, at Dylan's encouraging smile, at the casual way they'd all accepted my presence and expertise. These weren't irresponsible pranksters looking for someone else to do their work. They were genuinely talented students who'd encountered a challenging magical problem and wanted to collaborate on a solution.

It was exactly the kind of intellectual challenge I'd always loved.

"I suppose," I said slowly, "I could take a look at your spell framework. Purely for academic interest, you understand."

"Academic interest," Jasper repeated with a knowing smile. "Of course."

"But," I continued, "if I'm going to help with something this complex, we're going to do it properly. Full magical theory backing, safety protocols, and absolutely no spell-casting unless we're certain we can control the results."

"Yes, ma'am," Finn said with mock solemnity.

"And someone needs to research whether there are any historical precedents for animating university architecture. I refuse to accidentally trigger some kind of institutional protection ward."

"I'll handle that," Kieran volunteered.

"Good. Dylan, I'll need detailed measurements of each gargoyle's magical resonance patterns."

"On it," Dylan said, grinning.

"And if anyone asks, this is a theoretical exercise in advanced collaborative magic. We are not planning to actually perform unauthorized enchantments on university property."

"Understood," they chorused.

As the conversation shifted to technical details and magical theory, I found myself pulled into the kind of collaborative problem-solving I'd always loved but rarely had the opportunity to experience. The fox shifters approached magic with a creativity and flexibility that complemented my more structured analytical approach perfectly.

It felt like partnership magic on a larger scale.

About an hour later, as the fire burned down to comfortable coals and the evening air grew cooler, I found myself sitting between Dylan and Kieran, debating the finer points of gargoyle animation theory while Finn sketched spell diagrams in the dirt with a stick.

"You know," Jasper said during a pause in the technical discussion, "this is the most focused I've seen these guys in months."

"Academic rigor is contagious," I replied, then realized how formal that sounded. "I mean—"

"She means we're all nerds at heart," Dylan said with affection. "We just express it differently."

"Some of us express it through elaborate pranks," Kieran added.

"Some of us express it through turning theoretical magic into spectacular demonstrations," Finn chimed in.

"And some of us," I said, surprising myself with the ease of the response, "express it by figuring out how to make impossible things possible."

"That," Jasper said with satisfaction, "sounds like exactly the kind of approach this group needs."

As the gathering began to wind down, various fox shifters drifting back toward the residence hall, I realized I was genuinely reluctant to leave. The easy camaraderie, the intellectual stimulation, the way they'd welcomed me not as Dylan's girlfriend or Professor Lumina's protégé but simply as Lyra—it was everything I hadn't known I'd been missing.

"So," Dylan said as we walked back toward the main campus together, "what did you think?"

"They're not what I expected," I admitted.

"Disappointed?"

"The opposite." I looked back toward Reynard Hall, where warm lights still glowed in several windows. "They're brilliant. And kind. And they accepted me without any of the usual academic posturing."

"They did, didn't they?" Dylan's voice carried a note of pleased surprise. "Though I have to say, I've never seen them get so excited about spell theory before."

"The gargoyle opera is genuinely impressive work. Complex enough to challenge graduate students."

"And you're really going to help them figure it out?"

I considered the question. A week ago, the answer would have been an immediate no. Unauthorized magical experimentation, potential property damage, possible academic consequences—too many variables, too much risk.

Now, thinking about the way Kieran's eyes had lit up when I'd explained resonance pattern theory, or how Finn had immediately grasped the implications of compound animation charms, I found my perspective had shifted.

"I suppose I am," I said. "Though I maintain this is purely theoretical research."

Dylan's laughter echoed across the quiet campus. "Of course it is."

"It is," I insisted, then paused. "Dylan?"

"Yeah?"

"Thank you. For introducing me to them. For letting me be part of this."

Dylan stopped walking and turned to face me, his expression serious in the moonlight. "Lyra, you don't need my permission to be part of anything. They liked you because you're amazing, not because you're with me."

"But if you hadn't invited me—"

"Then I would have been an idiot who kept the best part of his life separate from his family." Dylan's expression grew more vulnerable. "I was afraid you'd think they were too wild, or that I was. That maybe you'd see this part of me and decide I wasn't... enough."

Dylan reached up to tuck a strand of hair behind my ear. "I should be thanking you for being brave enough to trust me with this."

Standing there in the quiet evening air, surrounded by the familiar spires of NPU but feeling like I was seeing everything with new eyes, I realized something important had shifted.

Professor Lumina had valued achievement above all else. Our dinners had been quiet, formal affairs—conversations about academic milestones and research goals, expectations outlined with the precision of mathematical proofs. No laughter, no bonfires, no card games around enchanted furniture. Certainly no acceptance based on anything as simple as being yourself.

Though I understood why Professor Lumina had raised me with such structured discipline—she'd wanted me to succeed in a world that didn't easily accept magical orphans—I'd never experienced the warmth of belonging simply for who I was.

For the first time in years, I felt like I belonged somewhere beyond the confines of academic achievement.

I felt like I had found my own chosen family.

And maybe, just maybe, that was the most magical discovery of all.

CHAPTER TEN
THE TRICKSTER STRIKES

DYLAN

The first sign of trouble came three days after Lyra's visit to the Fox Den, when I arrived at Advanced Shifting Theory to find Professor Moonheart looking like someone had stolen her favorite crystal ball.

"Mr. Vixen," she said before I'd even fully entered the classroom, "please remain after class. We need to discuss some concerning developments."

My stomach dropped. In my experience, "concerning developments" was academic code for "you're in deep trouble and we have evidence."

The class proceeded with the usual mix of theoretical discussion and practical exercises, but I found it impossible to concentrate. My shifting practice was even more unstable than usual—my fox form kept flickering with nervous energy, tail refusing to maintain proper proportions. By the time Professor Moonheart dismissed the other students, I was pretty sure I'd failed whatever assessment we'd been doing.

"Dylan," Professor Moonheart said once we were alone, "I'm going to ask you a direct question, and I need you to answer honestly. Have you been involved in any unauthorized magical experimentation lately?"

Define unauthorized, I thought, but managed to keep my expression neutral. "What kind of experimentation?"

"The kind that might destabilize existing enchantments on campus." Her silver eyes were sharp, searching. "Several professors have reported irregularities in their classroom protection wards. Fluctuations that suggest someone has been testing partnership magic applications."

My blood went cold. "Partnership magic?"

"Don't play innocent, Dylan. Your... tutoring arrangement with Miss Lumina has been noticed. As has the fact that you've been spending considerable time in areas of campus where you have no academic reason to be."

"I haven't done anything wrong," I said, which was technically true if you ignored the whole "planning to enchant architectural elements" thing.

"Perhaps not intentionally. But partnership magic is dangerous, Dylan. Unpredictable. There's a reason it fell out of practice centuries ago."

"What reason?"

Professor Moonheart studied me for a long moment. "Because partnerships can become dependencies. Because magical bonds, once formed, can be difficult to break. And because the kind of power generated by true magical partnerships has historically proven... difficult for institutions to regulate."

The way she said "regulate" made it sound distinctly ominous.

"Are you telling me to stop working with Lyra?"

"I'm telling you to be careful. Very careful. There are members of the faculty who believe partnership magic research should be suspended entirely." She gathered her materials with sharp, precise movements. "I suggest you and Miss Lumina conduct your studies with considerably more discretion."

I left her classroom with my mind racing. Someone was watching us. Someone had noticed the magical fluctuations our partnership was creating. And someone thought we were dangerous enough to warrant an official warning.

The question was: what were we going to do about it?

———

I FOUND Lyra in the Library of Lights, which had become our default meeting place since the hidden chamber discovery. She was surrounded by even more books than usual, her dark hair falling like a curtain as she bent over what looked like historical records of magical regulation policies.

"Research for our gargoyle project?" I asked, settling into the chair across from her.

"Research into why Professor Lumina has been asking pointed questions about my study schedule," Lyra replied without looking up. "And why the Dean of Magical Studies requested a meeting with me next week."

My stomach sank further. "They're pressuring you too?"

"Professor Moonheart?"

"She knows about the partnership magic. Says there are faculty members who want the research suspended."

Lyra finally looked up, and I could see worry etched across her features. "This is what I was afraid of. Dylan, what if we've pushed too far, too fast? What if the magical fluctuations we've been creating are actually dangerous?"

"Are they?"

"I don't know," she admitted, and the uncertainty in her voice was more unsettling than any direct warning. "I've been going through historical records, trying to find precedents for what we're experiencing. Most of the partnership magic documentation was deliberately obscured or removed from the archives."

"Removed by whom?"

"That's what's concerning me. According to these administrative records, there was a systematic purge of partnership magic research in the late 1800s. Official reason: 'Protecting students from unstable magical practices.'"

"And the unofficial reason?"

Lyra's expression was grim. "Fear. Partnership magic was becoming too powerful, too independent of institutional control. Students were forming bonds that superseded their loyalty to the university structure."

I thought about the way our magic felt when it connected— wild, free, unlimited by the careful constraints that governed individual spellwork. If we could teach others to access that kind of power...

"They're afraid we'll start a revolution," I said slowly.

"They're afraid we'll prove that everything they've built their authority on is fundamentally flawed." Lyra closed the book she'd been reading with a sharp snap. "Dylan, what if they try to separate us? What if they decide our partnership is too dangerous to continue?"

The thought hit me like a physical blow. Lose Lyra? Lose the connection that had finally made my magic make sense, that had made me feel complete for the first time in my life?

"They can't do that," I said, but even as the words left my mouth, I knew they weren't true. The administration could do whatever they wanted—reassign tutoring partnerships, restrict access to certain areas of campus, even suspend students for "unauthorized magical experimentation."

"Actually," a new voice said from behind us, "they can. And they're already planning to."

We both spun around to find Marcus Evergreen approaching our table, his silver hair catching the magical lighting in a way that made him look older, more serious than usual.

"Marcus?" Lyra's voice was carefully neutral. "What are you doing here?"

"Warning you." Marcus glanced around the library, then moved closer and lowered his voice. "My father is on the Board of Magical Regulation. They've received a formal complaint about unauthorized partnership magic research being conducted at NPU."

"A complaint from whom?" I asked, though I was pretty sure I didn't want to know the answer.

"Professor Arcturus from the Winter Court." Marcus's expression was apologetic but determined. "Apparently, word has reached certain... interested parties about your discovery of the hidden chamber. They're claiming that partnership magic research represents a threat to the established magical hierarchy."

Lyra went very pale. "The Winter Court is involved?"

"Who's Professor Arcturus?" I asked, though the name stirred something uncomfortable in my memory.

"The same Professor Arcturus who sent me to NPU in the first place," Marcus said quietly. "Dylan, he's the one who's been... monitoring your academic progress since you arrived."

The pieces clicked together with sickening clarity. The mysterious benefactor who'd ensured my acceptance despite mediocre grades. The subtle pressure to excel academically. The way certain professors seemed to know more about my magical difficulties than I'd ever told them.

"He's been watching me," I said.

"He's been watching both of you," Marcus corrected. "The partnership magic discovery was apparently the trigger he was waiting for."

"Trigger for what?" Lyra demanded.

Marcus hesitated, then seemed to come to a decision. "For proving that partnership magic is inherently unstable and dangerous. For having you both expelled from NPU as a warning to other students who might be tempted to explore forbidden magical practices."

The words hit the air like a curse. Expelled. Separated. Everything we'd discovered, everything we'd built together, destroyed because someone else was afraid of what we represented.

"Marcus," Lyra said quietly, "why are you telling us this? You could get in serious trouble for sharing Board information."

Marcus's expression grew conflicted. "Because my father didn't always think this way. He used to tell stories about the old partnerships, before the regulation crackdowns. Said they were the most beautiful magic he'd ever witnessed." His voice dropped. "He changed after he joined the Winter Court. Started believing that the magical hierarchy was more important than magical freedom. I don't want to see you two become casualties of his... evolution."

"There has to be something we can do," I said desperately.

"There is," Marcus replied. "But you're not going to like it."

"What?"

"Stop. Completely. End the partnership magic research, avoid each other except for supervised tutoring sessions, and hope they decide you've learned your lesson."

"No." The word came out flat, final. "Absolutely not."

"Dylan—" Lyra began.

"No," I repeated, standing up so quickly my chair scraped

against the floor. "I'm not giving this up. I'm not giving you up. Not because some ancient politician is afraid that students might discover they don't need institutional permission to be powerful."

"Keep your voice down," Marcus hissed, glancing around nervously.

But I was beyond caring about discretion. "This is exactly what they want, isn't it? For us to be so scared of consequences that we police ourselves. Well, I'm done being scared."

"Dylan, please," Lyra said, reaching for my hand. "Maybe Marcus is right. Maybe we should step back, be more careful—"

"Be more careful?" I stared at her in disbelief. "Lyra, three days ago you were helping my friends plan elaborate magical pranks. You were laughing, being yourself, discovering what it felt like to belong somewhere. Are you really going to let them take that away?"

"I'm trying to protect what we have," she said quietly.

"By hiding it? By pretending it doesn't exist?"

"By being smart about it."

"Smart." I laughed, but there was no humor in the sound. "You know what's smart, Lyra? Recognizing that some things are worth fighting for."

I turned to leave, then paused and looked back at Marcus. "Tell your father and his Winter Court friends that if they want to stop us, they're going to have to do better than anonymous complaints and intimidation tactics."

"Dylan, wait—" Lyra called after me, but I was already walking away.

I needed air. I needed space to think. And I needed to figure out how to protect the most important thing that had ever happened to me without losing the person who made it matter in the first place.

. . .

I FOUND myself on the roof of Frost Hall, which had become my go-to spot for processing complicated emotions ever since I'd discovered the access stairway during freshman year. The gargoyles were silent now, their enchantment dormant, but I could still feel the residual magic from our recent prank experiments.

Partnership magic is dangerous, Professor Moonheart had said. *Difficult to regulate.*

Maybe that was exactly the point.

I was so lost in thought that I almost missed the sound of footsteps on the roof access stairs. Almost missed the familiar scent of winter air and structured magic that meant Lyra had followed me.

"Dylan," she said softly, approaching with the careful steps of someone who wasn't sure of their welcome.

"Come to tell me that Marcus is right?" I asked without turning around. "That we should give up everything we've discovered because it makes other people uncomfortable?"

"I came to apologize." Lyra moved to stand beside me at the roof's edge, close enough that I could feel the warmth of her presence. "And to tell you that you're right."

I finally looked at her. "I am?"

"About fighting for things that matter. About not letting fear make our decisions for us." She was quiet for a moment, staring out at the campus spread below us. "I spent so many years being careful, Dylan. Following rules, meeting expectations, never taking risks that might jeopardize my academic standing. And you know what I accomplished?"

"Revolutionary magical research?"

"Loneliness," she said simply. "I accomplished a lot of loneliness. Until I met you."

Something tight in my chest began to ease.

"I don't want to go back to that," Lyra continued. "I don't want to pretend that what we have is just tutoring, or that our magic doesn't make everything brighter, or that I haven't fallen completely in love with a fox shifter who makes me brave enough to enchant gargoyles and crash bonfire gatherings."

My heart stopped. "Did you just—?"

"Say I love you?" Lyra turned to face me fully, her pale eyes bright with determination. "Yes. I did. And if Professor Arcturus and the Winter Court don't like it, they can—what's the technical term?—bite me."

I stared at her for a moment, then started laughing. "Did Lyra Lumina just tell the Winter Court to bite her?"

"I believe I did."

"And did you just say you love me?"

"I believe I did that too."

I reached for her hands, pulling her closer. "For the record, I love you too. Completely, desperately, and probably since the moment you saved my magical ass in Professor Lumina's exam."

"That long?"

"Probably longer." I touched my forehead to hers. "Lyra, whatever they throw at us—"

"We'll face it together," she finished. "Partners."

"Partners."

And then, finally, inevitably, I kissed her.

It was supposed to be soft, tentative, a first kiss that acknowledged everything that had been building between us. Instead, it was magic. Literal magic. The moment our lips touched, power flared around us—not the chaotic energy of my usual spellwork or the controlled precision of hers, but something entirely new. Something that belonged to both of us and neither of us, something that sang with harmony and possibility.

The gargoyles around us stirred to life, not with the controlled animation of our planned enchantments but with something spontaneous and joyful. They began to sing—not opera, but something that sounded like celebration, like recognition, like the universe itself applauding.

When we finally broke apart, breathing hard, the entire campus was lit up with aurora patterns that definitely hadn't been there moments before.

"Did we just—?" Lyra began.

"Create a massive magical display visible from orbit?" I finished. "Probably."

From somewhere below us, I heard voices—students emerging from buildings to stare up at the impossible light show, professors' concerned murmurs drifting up from the courtyard.

"Look at those patterns!" someone called out. "They're moving like they're alive!"

"Is that coming from Frost Hall?" another voice asked.

One of the gargoyles chose that moment to pipe up with what sounded suspiciously like a cheerful wolf whistle, and I winced.

"They're definitely going to know about this," Lyra said.

"Let them know." I cupped her face in my hands, marveling at the way her eyes reflected the dancing lights we'd accidentally created. "Let everyone know. I'm done hiding what you mean to me."

Lyra's smile was radiant. "Then I suppose we'd better make sure we're ready for whatever comes next."

"Any ideas about how we do that?"

"Actually," she said, her expression shifting into the focused intensity I recognized as her problem-solving mode, "I might have a few. But first, I think we need to have a conversation with your Fox Den friends about accelerating our gargoyle project timeline."

"Why?"

"Because if they're going to try to stop us from researching

partnership magic, I want to give them something really spectacular to complain about first."

I grinned. "I knew there was a reason I fell in love with you."

"Just one reason?"

"Well," I said, pulling her closer as the aurora lights continued
to dance around us, "maybe a few hundred. But your vengeful
streak definitely made the list."

As we stood there on the roof, surrounded by singing
gargoyles and impossible lights, planning what was probably
going to be the most elaborate magical prank in NPU history, I
realized that maybe the administration was right to be worried.

Partnership magic was dangerous.

It was dangerous to anyone who profited from keeping
magical students isolated, competitive, and dependent on institutional approval.

And we were about to prove just how dangerous it could be.

CHAPTER ELEVEN

ILLUMINATION

LYRA

The emergency faculty meeting was called for eight o'clock the morning after our kiss lit up half the campus. I knew because Professor Lumina's usually composed demeanor had developed stress fractures around the edges, and she'd been pacing the Observatory since dawn.

"Lyra," she said without preamble when I arrived for what was supposed to be our regular research session, "we need to discuss what happened last night."

"You mean the aurora display?" I tried for academic neutrality, but my voice betrayed me with a slight tremor.

"I mean the unauthorized magical experiment that created a campus-wide phenomenon visible from three neighboring towns." Professor Lumina's pale eyes were sharp with something that might have been concern or might have been disappointment. "The kind of magical working that draws attention from regulatory bodies we'd prefer to avoid."

My stomach clenched. "Professor, if this is about the partnership magic research—"

"This is about the fact that you and Mr. Vixen have apparently progressed beyond research into active magical bonding." She moved to the Observatory's eastern window, gazing out at the campus where maintenance crews were still trying to figure out why several buildings were glowing with residual aurora energy. "Do you have any idea what you've done?"

"Created a beautiful magical display?" I said weakly.

"You've announced to everyone with magical sensitivity within a fifty-mile radius that two students at North Pole University have achieved active partnership bonding." Professor Lumina turned back to face me, and her expression was more serious than I'd ever seen it. "Lyra, there are people who would kill to study a bond like yours. And others who would kill to destroy it."

The casual mention of killing made my blood run cold. "Professor, when you say 'bonding'—are we talking about something permanent? Something that can't be undone?"

"Partnership bonds exist on a spectrum," Professor Lumina explained carefully. "What you and Dylan experienced last night was the beginning of true magical integration—deeper than simple compatibility, but not yet the permanent soul-bond that takes years to fully develop. Think of it as... magical engagement rather than marriage."

"But it can still be broken?"

"Forcibly separating an emerging bond is extremely dangerous and often traumatic. The magical backlash alone..." She shook her head. "Let's just say there's good reason the practice was banned after the Regulation Wars." "Surely you're exaggerating—"

"Am I? Tell me, what do you know about the Magical Regulation Wars of the 1890s?"

"They were... conflicts over standardization of magical education?" I'd read about them briefly, but they'd always seemed like ancient history.

"They were systematic attempts to eliminate partnership magic from magical society," Professor Lumina corrected grimly. "Hundreds of bonded pairs were forcibly separated. Some died from the magical backlash. Others went into hiding and were never seen again."

I sank into the nearest chair as the implications hit me. "You think someone might try to separate Dylan and me by force?"

"I think Professor Arcturus has already begun making arrangements to do exactly that." Professor Lumina moved to her desk and activated a privacy ward with sharp, efficient gestures. "Which is why we need to accelerate your training significantly."

"Training for what?"

"For defending your bond." She pulled out several ancient texts I'd never seen before, their covers marked with symbols that seemed to shift and dance when I looked at them directly. "Partnership magic isn't just about combining individual abilities, Lyra. True bonded pairs can access forms of magic that individual casters cannot touch."

My pulse quickened with a mixture of excitement and terror. "What kind of magic?"

"The kind that made the Winter Court afraid enough to spend two centuries trying to eliminate it." Professor Lumina opened the first book, revealing pages covered with diagrams that looked more like mystical art than academic instruction. "Lyra, I'm about to tell you something that could put both of us in considerable danger. Are you certain you want to proceed?"

I thought about Dylan's determined expression when he'd refused to hide our connection. About the way his magic felt like coming home. About the possibility that someone might try to take that away from us.

"Yes," I said firmly. "Tell me everything."

Professor Lumina's smile was proud and worried in equal measure. "Very well. But first, we need to retrieve Mr. Vixen. If you're going to learn to defend your bond, you'll need to do it together."

———

TWENTY MINUTES LATER, Dylan arrived at the Observatory looking like he'd slept about as well as I had, which was to say not at all. His rust-colored hair was more disheveled than usual, and there were dark circles under his green eyes.

"Let me guess," he said as he settled into his usual chair, "we're in trouble."

"Considerable trouble," Professor Lumina confirmed. "But also considerable opportunity. Lyra, would you explain what we've discussed?"

I gave Dylan a rapid summary of the Regulation Wars, Professor Arcturus's likely intentions, and the revelation that partnership magic could access abilities beyond individual casting. By the time I finished, Dylan looked like he was processing information that fundamentally challenged everything he thought he knew about magic.

"So when we kissed last night and accidentally lit up the campus," he said slowly, "we weren't just creating a pretty light show. We were demonstrating the kind of power that historically gets people disappeared."

"Essentially, yes," Professor Lumina said. "Though I must say, the aurora display was remarkably sophisticated for an untrained bonded pair. Which brings us to today's lesson."

She gestured, and the Observatory's main display system acti-vated, showing not the theoretical models we'd been working with but something that looked like a combat training simulation.

"Today, you're going to learn active partnership casting under pressure," Professor Lumina announced. "Because if Professor Arcturus moves against you, academic theory won't be sufficient to protect your bond."

"Active partnership casting?" Dylan looked simultaneously intrigued and nervous. "What does that involve?"

"It involves you accessing magical abilities you've never successfully used before," Professor Lumina replied. "Lyra, you mentioned that Mr. Vixen's chaos magic organizes itself around your structured patterns. Today, we're going to test whether that effect works in reverse."

"What do you mean?" I asked.

"I mean we're going to see if your light magic can help Dylan access abilities that individual casting has never allowed him to reach." Professor Lumina's expression grew intense. "Dylan, have you ever successfully performed light magic?"

"Not really. I can manage basic color changes, but anything more complex..." Dylan shrugged helplessly. "It's never been my strong suit."

"Because you've been trying to cast it individually," Professor Lumina said. "Lyra, I want you to help him attempt something more challenging."

"How challenging?" I asked, though I suspected I already knew the answer.

"I want him to create sustained light constructs. The kind typically reserved for advanced graduate-level studies."

Dylan stared at her. "That's impossible. I can barely manage basic illumination spells."

"Not impossible," Professor Lumina corrected. "Impossible for individual casting given your magical signature. But partnership magic operates under different rules entirely."

She activated a section of the display that showed two human figures standing close together, their magical auras intertwining in complex patterns.

"True partnership casting doesn't just stabilize chaotic magic," she explained. "It allows each partner to access abilities that exist in the resonance space between their individual signatures. Dylan, your chaos magic combined with Lyra's structural precision could theoretically produce light constructs of extraordinary complexity."

"Theoretically," Dylan repeated dubiously.

"There's only one way to find out," I said, moving to stand beside him on the central platform. "Are you willing to try?"

Dylan looked at me, then at Professor Lumina, then back at me. "If this goes wrong and I accidentally destroy your Observatory, you're not allowed to be mad at me."

"Deal."

I took his hands, immediately feeling the familiar harmony as our magical signatures recognized each other. But instead of the gentle resonance we'd experienced before, Professor Lumina had apparently activated something in the Observatory's systems that amplified our connection.

The sensation was like stepping from a quiet room into a symphony hall mid-performance. Our combined magic didn't just flow together—it sang, creating harmonics I'd never imagined possible.

"Now," Professor Lumina instructed, "Dylan, I want you to visualize creating a light construct. Not just illumination, but solid light that can be shaped and maintained. Lyra, provide the structural framework he needs to make that visualization real."

I closed my eyes and reached for the mathematical principles underlying light manipulation theory. Instead of casting the magic myself, I tried to create a template that Dylan's chaotic energy could fill.

"I can feel it," Dylan said, wonder in his voice. "It's like... like having access to a language I never learned but somehow understand."

I opened my eyes and gasped.

Dylan was surrounded by light constructs of breathtaking complexity. Not the simple geometric shapes I typically created, but organic forms that seemed to grow and evolve as I watched. Crystalline flowers bloomed from his fingertips, their petals refracting rainbow patterns across the Observatory's walls. Birds made of pure radiance took flight around us, their wings leaving trails of golden fire.

But it wasn't just the technical sophistication that took my breath away. It was the artistry. Dylan's chaos magic, guided by my structural framework, was creating beauty unlike anything I'd ever seen.

"Dylan," I breathed, "this is incredible."

"It feels incredible," he replied, his voice filled with awe. "It feels like... like my magic finally makes sense."

Professor Lumina was watching with an expression of profound satisfaction. "Excellent. Now let's see if you can maintain the constructs while under stress."

Before either of us could ask what she meant, alarms began sounding throughout the Observatory. Not the gentle chimes of my usual notification system, but harsh, urgent warnings that meant immediate danger.

"What's happening?" Dylan asked, his light constructs flickering as his concentration wavered.

"Simulated attack," Professor Lumina said calmly. "In approximately thirty seconds, this room is going to be filled with hostile magical energy designed to disrupt partnership bonds. Your task is to maintain your light magic working despite the interference."

"You could have warned us!" I protested.

"Real attacks don't come with warnings," Professor Lumina replied. "Dylan, concentrate. Don't let the external pressure break your connection to the magic."

The first wave of disruptive energy hit like a sledgehammer to my magical senses. Every instinct screamed at me to break the connection with Dylan, to retreat into individual casting where I could maintain better control.

Dylan's light constructs immediately began destabilizing, their beautiful organic forms dissolving into chaotic swirls of energy.

"I can't hold it," Dylan said through gritted teeth. "It's too much—"

"Yes, you can," I said fiercely, tightening my grip on his hands. "Dylan, look at me."

His green eyes met mine, and I saw fear there, but also determination.

"You are brilliant," I told him, pushing every ounce of conviction I possessed into my voice. "Your magic isn't broken or defective. It's evolutionary. It's designed for this. And right now, I need you to trust it."

"Trust it?"

"Trust us."

Another wave of disruptive energy crashed over us, stronger than the first. This time, instead of fighting it, Dylan did something I'd never seen him do before. He embraced the chaos.

His magic exploded outward, not in the uncontrolled burst I'd witnessed during our first tutoring session, but in a deliberate, magnificent display of power channeled through my structural framework. The light constructs didn't just stabilize—they evolved, becoming more complex, more beautiful, more impossible.

The disruptive energy meant to break our bond was absorbed into Dylan's casting, becoming part of the pattern instead of destroying it. What should have been an attack became fuel for even more spectacular magic.

"Remarkable," Professor Lumina murmured, deactivating the simulation. "Dylan, do you understand what you just accomplished?"

Dylan stared at the light constructs still dancing around us, his expression somewhere between wonder and disbelief. "I used light magic. Real light magic."

"You used advanced light magic," I corrected, amazed. "Dylan, those constructs are graduate-level complexity. Some of them are techniques I've never even attempted."

"How is that possible?"

"Because," Professor Lumina said with satisfaction, "you're not trying to force your magic into patterns it wasn't designed for anymore. You're allowing it to be what it actually is—one half of something extraordinary."

Dylan turned to look at me, and the expression on his face made my heart skip. "You really think I'm brilliant?"

"I think," I said, reaching up to touch his cheek, "that you're exactly the partner my magic has been waiting for. And I think anyone who tries to separate us is about to discover exactly how formidable we can be together."

"Speaking of which," Professor Lumina interrupted, "I believe you have some unfinished magical demonstrations to consider. Professor Ember mentioned your friends have been asking about advanced collaborative spellwork."

"Why?" Dylan asked.

"Because Professor Arcturus has called for an emergency review of your case. The hearing is scheduled for tomorrow evening." Professor Lumina's expression grew grim. "Which means you have approximately thirty-six hours to publicly demonstrate that partnership magic creates beauty rather than chaos."

"Thirty-six hours," I repeated, my mind already racing through the logistics. "That's not enough time to properly test all the spell integrations—"

"Then we'd better make sure we get it right the first time," Dylan said with a grin that was equal parts confidence and reckless determination. "Good thing I've got the most brilliant magical theorist in the school as my partner."

"And I've got the most naturally gifted chaos mage," I replied. "Though I'm starting to think 'chaos mage' isn't the right term anymore."

"What would you call it?"

I looked at the light constructs still glowing softly around us, at the way Dylan's magic had turned attack into art, disruption into beauty.

"Revolutionary," I said. "I'd call it revolutionary."

And as we began planning what was probably going to be the most spectacular magical demonstration in NPU history, I realized that's exactly what we were becoming.

Revolutionaries who happened to be in love.

Outside the Observatory's windows, faint aurora patterns still shimmered in the upper spires of the campus buildings, silent witnesses to the kiss that had changed everything. And somewhere below, I could see clusters of students gathered in the courtyards, their animated conversations and pointing gestures making it clear that word of last night's display was spreading faster than winter wildfire.

By tomorrow's hearing, everyone would have chosen a side. The question was: would anyone choose ours?

CHAPTER TWELVE
EMOTIONAL BURN

DYLAN

The emergency faculty meeting was held in the Crystal Amphitheater, NPU's most formal academic space, which told me everything I needed to know about how seriously the administration was taking our "situation." I'd been summoned via official notice delivered by a nervous-looking administrative sprite who'd practically vibrated with anxiety while handing over the crystalline message tablet.

"Mr. Vixen," the notice had read in Professor Blitzen's characteristically crisp handwriting, "your presence is required at an emergency faculty review regarding recent unauthorized magical activities. This is not optional."

So here I was, sitting in one of the amphitheater's lower tiers while what looked like the entire NPU faculty arranged themselves in the elevated seating above me. It felt disturbingly like being on trial, which I supposed was exactly the point.

I'd faced disciplinary meetings before—pranks, missed assignments, the occasional magical mishap—but this felt different. This wasn't about grades or minor infractions. This was about Lyra. About us. About the possibility that they might try to take away the most important thing that had ever happened to me.

Professor Lumina sat in the front row, her expression carefully neutral, but her posture radiating protective tension. Professor Moonheart was there too, along with the heads of every major department. Even Professor Ember from Elemental Theory had shown up, her usual fiery demeanor replaced by something that looked like grim fascination.

And presiding over it all, in the amphitheater's central position of authority, was a figure I'd never seen before but recognized immediately from Marcus's descriptions: Professor Arcturus.

He was exactly what I'd expected the Winter Court's representative to look like—tall, pale, ageless in the way that suggested centuries of magical preservation, with silver hair that seemed to move in a breeze only he could feel. His ice-blue eyes swept the assembled faculty before settling on me with the weight of absolute judgment.

"Mr. Vixen," he said, his voice carrying easily through the amphitheater's acoustics, "thank you for joining us on such short notice."

Politeness didn't mask the command beneath it.

"Professor," I replied, trying to match his formal tone while fighting the urge to fidget under the collective stare of thirty faculty members.

"I'm sure you're wondering why we've called this emergency session," Professor Arcturus continued smoothly. "Recent events have raised serious concerns about unauthorized magical experimentation being conducted on campus. Specifically, experiments involving partnership magic—a field of study that has been restricted for very good reasons."

"Restricted by whom?" I asked before I could stop myself.

Faculty murmured, unease skimming the air. Apparently, questioning the Winter Court's authority wasn't the expected response.

Professor Arcturus's smile was cold and sharp. "By those with the wisdom to understand that some magical practices are too dangerous for unsupervised student exploration. Partnership magic has a documented history of instability, unpredictable effects, and tragic consequences."

"Tragic consequences for whom?" Professor Lumina's voice cut through the tension like a blade. "For the students who achieved extraordinary magical breakthroughs, or for the institutions that couldn't control them?"

The temperature in the amphitheater seemed to drop several degrees.

"Professor Lumina," Professor Arcturus said with dangerous politeness, "I hardly think this is the time for historical revisionism."

Professor Moonheart frowned, her fingers tapping restlessly on her armrest. Professor Blitzen shifted in his seat but said nothing. Only Professor Lumina met Arcturus's gaze head-on, silent but unflinching.

"Isn't it?" Professor Lumina rose from her seat with fluid grace. "Mr. Vixen, would you please demonstrate the light constructs you achieved yesterday?"

I blinked. "Here? Now?"

"Here and now."

I looked around at the faculty members watching me with expressions ranging from curiosity to barely concealed hostility. Creating magical demonstrations under pressure was not exactly my forte, especially without Lyra's stabilizing presence.

"I'm not sure that's a good idea—"

"I think it's an excellent idea," Professor Lumina said firmly. "After all, Professor Arcturus seems convinced that partnership magic produces only chaos and destruction. Perhaps we should let the evidence speak for itself."

The challenge hung in the air like a drawn sword. I could feel the weight of expectation from every direction—Professor Lumina's faith, Professor Arcturus's skepticism, the faculty's professional curiosity.

And underneath it all, my own desperate need to prove that what Lyra and I had discovered was worth defending.

I closed my eyes and reached for the memory of yesterday's breakthrough—the way Lyra's structured magic had provided the framework for my chaos to flow through. But without her physical presence, without the harmony of our combined magical signatures, the advanced light magic remained frustratingly out of reach.

What emerged instead was a handful of basic illumination orbs, pretty but hardly revolutionary.

"Interesting," Professor Arcturus said with satisfaction. "It seems Mr. Vixen's supposedly remarkable abilities require the presence of his... partner to function. How remarkably dependent."

Heat flooded my cheeks. "It's not dependency. It's collaboration—"

"It's dangerous entanglement," Professor Arcturus corrected coldly. "The kind of unhealthy magical relationship that historically leads to psychological instability and, in extreme cases, complete magical collapse when the partnership is severed."

"That's not—" I started, but the amphitheater doors chose that moment to swing open with a crystalline chime.

Lyra stepped through, her dark hair slightly disheveled and her blue robes skewed, breath still catching like she'd run across campus. Her pale eyes immediately found mine, and I felt something tight in my chest ease at her presence.

"I'm sorry I'm late," she said, not sounding sorry at all. "I was under the impression this was a faculty meeting, not a student tribunal."

"Miss Lumina," Professor Arcturus said with cold politeness, "how good of you to join us. We were just discussing the concerning developments in your... research partnership with Mr. Vixen."

"Were you?" Lyra moved down the amphitheater steps with the kind of controlled precision that meant she was furious and trying not to show it. "And what conclusions did you reach?"

"That partnership magic represents an unacceptable risk to student safety and institutional stability," Professor Arcturus replied smoothly. "I'm sure you understand our concerns."

"Actually, I don't." Lyra came to stand beside me, and immediately, I felt the familiar harmony as our magical signatures recognized each other. "Perhaps you could explain exactly what dangers you're so concerned about?"

"The dangers," Professor Arcturus said, his voice taking on the tone of someone delivering a lecture to particularly slow students, "of students forming magical dependencies that supersede their loyalty to established educational structures. The dangers of magical bonds that cannot be properly supervised or regulated. The dangers of—"

"The dangers of students discovering they don't need institutional permission to be powerful?" Lyra interrupted, her voice carrying clearly through the amphitheater.

The silence that followed was deafening.

"Miss Lumina," Professor Blitzen said carefully, "surely you're not suggesting that students should pursue unauthorized magical experimentation without faculty oversight?"

"I'm suggesting," Lyra said, her chin lifting with defiant determination, "that some discoveries are too important to be limited by administrative fear. Dylan and I haven't just rediscovered partnership magic—we've proven that magical education's foundational assumptions about individual casting superiority are wrong."

She gestured, and the amphitheater's display system activated, showing holographic projections of our magical signature interactions.

"Look at these resonance patterns," she continued, falling into her academic presentation mode despite the hostile audience. "Partnership magic doesn't just add individual abilities together —it creates exponential enhancement. Dylan's chaos magic provides creative flexibility that my structured approach could never achieve alone. My theoretical framework gives his intuitive casting the precision it needs to reach its full potential."

"Interesting theory," Professor Arcturus said dismissively. "But hardly evidence of—"

"Dylan," Lyra said quietly, turning to face me, "show them what we accomplished yesterday."

This time, with Lyra's presence stabilizing my magical core, the advanced light constructs came easily. But instead of the organic beauty I'd created in the Observatory, I found myself crafting something different—geometric patterns that spoke to mathematical precision while maintaining the flowing creativity that was uniquely mine.

The light constructs that bloomed around us weren't just technically sophisticated. They were a perfect fusion of our magical approaches, chaos and order dancing together in patterns that neither of us could have achieved alone.

A collective intake of breath echoed through the amphitheater.

"Remarkable," Professor Moonheart murmured.

"Graduate-level complexity," Professor Ember added, leaning forward with obvious interest.

"And achieved by two sophomore students working in partnership," Professor Lumina said with quiet satisfaction.

Professor Arcturus's expression had gone dangerously cold. "Impressive theatrics," he said dismissively. "But magical flashiness doesn't address the fundamental concerns about partnership magic's long-term stability."

"What concerns, specifically?" Lyra challenged.

"The concern that students who form these... bonds become increasingly isolated from normal academic and social structures. The concern that magical partnerships create insular relationships that resist external guidance. The concern that—"

"The concern that we might realize we don't need you," I said, the words coming out before I could stop them.

The amphitheater went dead silent.

Professor Arcturus's smile was arctic. "How refreshingly honest. Yes, Mr. Vixen, that is indeed the concern. Students who believe they can pursue magical education without proper supervision, without institutional guidance, without respect for the wisdom of their betters."

"Our betters?" Lyra's voice carried a dangerous edge. "You mean the same institutional wisdom that spent two centuries suppressing one of the most powerful forms of magic ever discovered? The same supervision that would rather maintain control than allow students to reach their full potential?"

"Miss Lumina," Professor Blitzen warned, "you're treading on very dangerous ground."

"Good," Lyra shot back. "Maybe it's time someone did."

She stepped forward, addressing the entire assembled faculty with the kind of academic authority that I'd seen her use during tutoring sessions but never in direct confrontation with professors.

"Partnership magic works," she said, her voice ringing with conviction. "It works better than individual casting for students whose magical signatures are compatible. It produces stronger magic, more stable spell-work, and more creative applications than anything our current educational model can achieve."

"And the risks—" Professor Arcturus began.

"Are manageable with proper understanding," Lyra cut him off. "The historical tragedies you keep referencing weren't caused by partnership magic itself. They were caused by the forced separation of established bonds. By institutions that would rather destroy student partnerships than admit they might need to change their teaching methods."

She gestured again, and the display shifted to show historical documents I recognized from her recent research.

"Every documented case of 'partnership magic instability' can be traced back to external interference. Students whose bonds were forcibly severed. Partners who were separated by an institutional decree. Magical compatibility that was treated as a problem to be solved rather than a gift to be developed."

Professor Arcturus's composure was finally beginning to crack. "Miss Lumina, you are advocating for a complete restructuring of magical education based on the experiences of two students—"

"I'm advocating for allowing students to learn in the ways that work best for them," Lyra said fiercely. "I'm advocating for an educational system that enhances student abilities rather than limiting them to fit institutional convenience."

"And if the Board of Magical Regulation disagrees with your assessment?"

"Then the Board of Magical Regulation will have to explain

why they're more interested in maintaining control than in advancing magical understanding."

The silence that followed was heavy with tension and unspoken consequences.

Professor Arcturus rose from his seat with the fluid grace of someone accustomed to having the final word in any conversation.

"Miss Lumina," he said with deadly calm, "you have just advocated for educational policies that directly contradict established magical regulation. You have publicly challenged the authority of institutions that have maintained magical stability for centuries. And you have done so while defending research that violates multiple university policies."

"Yes," Lyra said simply. "I have."

"Then I'm afraid you leave me no choice." Professor Arcturus's smile was triumphant and cold. "Effective immediately, you are removed from all advanced magical research programs. Your access to university research facilities is suspended pending further review. And your tutoring arrangement with Mr. Vixen is permanently terminated."

The words hit like physical blows. Lyra's chin stayed high, but her hand trembled slightly in mine—a tiny betrayal of the storm beneath her calm exterior.

"You're punishing her for defending partnership magic?" I demanded, surging to my feet.

"I'm protecting the university from students who refuse to accept proper guidance," Professor Arcturus replied coolly. "Miss Lumina made her choice. Now she must live with the consequences."

"The consequences of what? Of proving that your 'proper guidance' is based on fear rather than wisdom?"

"The consequences of academic insubordination and violation

of university policy." Professor Arcturus gathered his materials with sharp, decisive movements. "This hearing is concluded. Miss Lumina, you will report to the Academic Review Board tomorrow morning to discuss your continued enrollment at this institution."

He strode from the amphitheater without another word, leaving behind a wake of stunned silence.

"Lyra," I said quietly, reaching for her hand.

She took it automatically, but her eyes were distant, processing the magnitude of what had just happened.

"They can't do this," I said desperately. "Professor Lumina, tell them they can't do this."

Professor Lumina's expression was grim. "I'm afraid they can, Dylan. And they just did."

"But she was defending something important. Something that could change magical education for the better."

"Yes," Professor Lumina agreed sadly. "Which is exactly why they're so determined to stop her."

As the faculty began filing out of the amphitheater, most avoiding eye contact, I realized that everything had changed. Not just for our research or our relationship, but for Lyra's entire future at NPU.

She'd risked everything to defend what we'd discovered together.

And now she might lose everything because of it.

The question was: what was I going to do about it?

LATER THAT EVENING, I found Lyra sitting alone in the Observatory, staring at research displays that were no longer officially hers to use. She'd changed out of her formal robes into simple clothes, and without the academic regalia, she looked younger, more vulnerable.

"Hey," I said softly, settling into the chair beside her.

"Hey, yourself." Her voice was steady, but I could hear the exhaustion underneath.

"How are you holding up?"

"I'm trying to figure out if I just made the biggest mistake of my academic career or the most important stand of my life."

I studied her profile in the soft aurora lighting of the Observatory. "Any conclusions?"

"Both, probably." She turned to face me, and I saw determination warring with fear in her pale eyes. "Dylan, I need you to know something. What I said in there—about partnership magic, about institutional control—I meant every word. Even knowing what it would cost me."

"I know you did."

"And I need you to know that I don't regret it. Even if they expel me, even if I lose my research privileges, even if I have to start over somewhere else—I don't regret defending what we have."

The fierce conviction in her voice made something warm unfurl in my chest.

"Lyra," I said carefully, "what if there was a way to prove them wrong? What if we could demonstrate that partnership magic creates beauty and stability instead of chaos and destruction?"

"How?"

"The gargoyle opera." I leaned forward, excitement building as the plan crystallized in my mind. "Tomorrow night, before your review board meeting. We perform it exactly as planned, but we make it bigger. More spectacular. More impossible to ignore."

"Dylan, if we get caught performing unauthorized magic after what happened today—"

"Then we make sure we don't get caught until it's too late to stop us." I reached for her hands, feeling the familiar harmony as our magic recognized each other. "Lyra, you said it yourself—partnership magic works. So let's prove it in a way they can't dismiss or suppress or regulate away."

"That's incredibly risky."

"Everything worthwhile is risky."

Lyra was quiet for a long moment, considering. Then, slowly, she began to smile.

"You know," she said thoughtfully, "I've always wondered what Phantom of the Opera would sound like when performed by magically animated architecture."

"Is that a yes?"

"That's a yes." Her smile turned mischievous. "Though I maintain this is for purely academic research purposes."

"Of course it is."

"And Dylan?"

"Yeah?"

"If we're going to do this, we're going to do it right. No half-measures, no backup plans, no safety nets."

"I wouldn't have it any other way."

As we began finalizing plans for what was probably going to be the most elaborate magical demonstration in NPU history, I realized that losing her research privileges might have been the worst mistake Professor Arcturus could have made.

Because now Lyra had nothing left to lose.

And a brilliant woman with nothing left to lose was the most dangerous kind of revolutionary.

She'd risked everything to defend what we'd discovered together. Now I had to decide: was I willing to risk everything to fight for her?

The answer, I realized, had never been in question.

CHAPTER THIRTEEN
ACCIDENTAL MAGIC MISHAP

LYRA

The Fox Den had been transformed into something between a war room and a magical laboratory. Enchanted diagrams covered every available surface, floating spell matrices hung in mid-air like three-dimensional blueprints, and someone had charmed the furniture to rearrange itself into optimal collaborative workspace configurations every few minutes.

It was a symphony of controlled chaos—and for once, I welcomed it.

Still, beneath the productive noise, a knot of tension curled in my stomach. This wasn't just another research project. This was a magical performance with everything—our reputations, our bond —on the line.

"Okay," Kieran said, consulting a floating checklist that occasionally tried to reorganize itself, "synchronization spells are ready, costume illusions are programmed, and Finn's managed to convince the kitchen sprites to provide fog effects that won't set off the fire suppression system."

"Status on pyrotechnics?" Dylan asked from where he was fine-tuning the magical resonance calculations I'd helped him design.

"Handled," Jasper replied with the satisfaction of someone who'd spent considerable time working out complex logistics. "Turns out Professor Ember was a theater major before she went into Elemental Studies. She's... enthusiastic about our project."

I looked up from the spell framework I'd been reviewing. "Professor Ember knows about this?"

"She knows we're planning a 'creative magical demonstration,'" Jasper said carefully. "She doesn't know it's happening tonight, or that it's specifically designed to prove partnership magic theory, or that we're doing it without official authorization."

"So she knows nothing important," Dylan summarized.

"Exactly."

I returned my attention to the magical matrices, but something nagged at me about the synchronization patterns. The spell framework was sound—not just sound, it was elegant, almost beautiful—but there was a complexity to coordinating eight different gargoyle animation sequences that made me nervous.

"Dylan," I said slowly, "have we tested the magical load distribution? I'm concerned about what happens when we're channeling this much energy through the partnership bond simultaneously."

Dylan moved to stand beside me, automatically taking my hand as he studied the floating diagrams. The moment our skin touched, the spell matrices responded, their patterns shifting to accommodate our combined magical signature.

"The calculations look solid," he said, but I caught the slight uncertainty in his voice. "Though I'll admit, we're working with theoretical maximums rather than tested parameters."

"Which means?"

"Which means tonight, we were the experiment," Finn said cheerfully. "Personally, I'm betting it can. You two have been creating impossible magic together for weeks."

"Impossible magic, yes," I said carefully. "But never anything this sustained or complex. Dylan, what we're planning requires maintaining an active magical connection for nearly twenty minutes while simultaneously coordinating multiple animation sequences, illusion overlays, and environmental effects."

"You're having second thoughts," Kieran observed.

"I'm having practical concerns about magical overload," I corrected. "Partnership bonds are powerful, but they're not infinite. Push too hard too fast, and the magical backlash could be dangerous."

"Dangerous how?" Dylan asked quietly.

I hesitated, running through the theoretical scenarios I'd researched. "Best case, temporary magical exhaustion and a very disappointed audience. Worst case..." I trailed off, not wanting to voice the possibility that had been keeping me awake.

"Worst case what, Lyra?"

"Worst case, we destabilize the bond entirely. Potentially permanently."

The Fox Den went very quiet.

"You mean we could lose our magical connection?" Dylan's voice was carefully controlled, but I could hear the fear underneath.

"It's a possibility. Magical bonds can be damaged by overextension, especially in the early stages of development." I looked around at the concerned faces watching us. "I should have mentioned this sooner, but I was hoping the calculations would show a larger safety margin."

"And they don't?"

"They show we'll be operating right at the theoretical limit." I gestured to the floating diagrams, highlighting the areas of concern. "If anything goes wrong—if we lose synchronization, if the gargoyles' magical signatures fluctuate, if we encounter any unexpected interference—the magical load could exceed our bond's capacity to handle it safely."

Jasper leaned back in his chair, studying the spell framework with the kind of analytical intensity that reminded me why he was considered one of the Den's most capable strategists.

"What if we scaled it back?" he suggested. "Fewer gargoyles, simpler effects, shorter duration?"

"Then it becomes a pretty magical demonstration instead of a revolutionary proof of partnership magic's potential," Dylan said flatly. "Jasper, after what happened today, we need this to be undeniable. Spectacular enough that they can't dismiss it, powerful enough that they can't ignore it."

"Dylan's right," I said reluctantly. "If we're going to prove that partnership magic creates beauty rather than chaos, we need to create something beautiful enough to change minds. Something that individual casting could never achieve."

"Even if it means risking your magical bond?" Kieran asked seriously.

Dylan and I looked at each other, and I saw my own conflicted feelings reflected in his green eyes. The partnership magic we'd discovered was precious beyond measure—it had transformed both our abilities and our understanding of what magic could be. The thought of potentially losing it was terrifying.

But the thought of letting Professor Arcturus win, of allowing partnership magic to be suppressed again for another century, was worse.

"Yes," I said quietly. "Even if it means risking the bond."

"Well," Dylan added with forced lightness, "what's the point of having revolutionary magic if you're too scared to use it revolutionarily?"

"That's not a word," I said automatically.

"Language evolves," he said, smug.

Despite everything, I found myself smiling. "Your approach to language is as chaotic as your approach to magic."

"And your approach to both is as structured as always. See? We balance each other perfectly."

The affection in his voice made something warm settle in my chest, even as anxiety continued to gnaw at the edges of my mind.

"Alright," Jasper said decisively. "If we're doing this, we're doing it right. Full effect, maximum impact, and we deal with whatever consequences come afterward."

"Agreed," Kieran said.

"Absolutely," Finn added.

They all looked at Dylan and me expectantly.

"Together?" Dylan asked, squeezing my hand gently.

"Together," I confirmed.

———

TWO HOURS LATER, we were positioned on the roof of Frost Hall, surrounded by the eight gargoyles that would serve as our performers. The night air was crisp and clear, perfect for the kind of magical acoustics we'd need for the opera to carry across campus.

"Final systems check," I announced, consulting the magical monitoring devices I'd brought from the Observatory. "Animation frameworks are stable, illusion overlays are loaded, synchronization matrix is active."

"Pyrotechnic effects ready," Finn reported.

"Fog generators primed," Kieran added.

"Emergency shutdown protocols activated," Jasper said, giving us all a meaningful look. "If anything starts going wrong, I'll trigger immediate magical dampening."

"Hopefully it won't come to that," Dylan said, but his tension was obvious in the set of his shoulders.

I moved to stand beside him at the center of our spell array, taking his hands in the familiar gesture that had become as natural as breathing.

"Ready?" I asked.

"Ready."

Together, we reached for our magic.

The initial connection was perfect—our magical signatures finding each other with the harmony we'd come to expect. The partnership bond flared to life around us, creating the stable foundation we'd need for the complex spellwork ahead.

Then we began activating the gargoyle animations.

The first three gargoyles came to life smoothly, their stone forms gaining the fluid grace necessary for theatrical performance. The fourth and fifth followed suit, their individual magical signatures integrating seamlessly with our control matrix.

But when we attempted to activate the sixth gargoyle, something went wrong.

Instead of the smooth integration we'd achieved with the others, the gargoyle's magical signature clashed with our partnership bond. The conflict created a feedback loop that sent chaotic energy ricocheting through the entire spell framework.

The air crackled with unstable energy, the harmony between our magic unraveling like thread pulled too tight. For the first time since discovering our bond, I felt it strain, felt the terrifying possibility that we might not hold it together.

"Dylan!" I called out as the magical matrix around us began destabilizing.

"I see it!" he replied, pouring more energy into the synchronization spells. "Can you compensate for the resonance conflict?"

I tried reaching deeper into our partnership bond to find the additional magical capacity we needed. But the gargoyle's resistance was stronger than anticipated, requiring more power than our calculations had accounted for.

The seventh and eighth gargoyles activated anyway, responding to the magical chaos rather than our deliberate control. Suddenly, we had six animated gargoyles performing completely different pieces of music while two others attempted acrobatic stunts that their stone forms were never designed for.

"This is getting out of hand," Kieran shouted over the cacophony.

"Jasper, hit the emergency shutdown!" I called back.

"I'm trying! The magical dampening isn't responding!"

The chaos was spreading. Our partnership bond, overloaded by the conflicting magical demands, was beginning to fluctuate wildly. I could feel Dylan's magic becoming erratic, his usual controlled chaos turning into something genuinely dangerous.

And then, just as I was about to suggest we abandon the spell entirely, Dylan did something unexpected.

Instead of fighting the chaos, he embraced it.

"Lyra," he said, his voice calm despite the magical storm raging around us, "stop trying to control the gargoyles individually. Let them find their own harmony."

"That's not how synchronized spellwork functions—"

"It's not how individual spellwork functions," Dylan corrected. "But partnership magic operates differently, remember? Trust the connection."

Against every instinct I possessed, I loosened my grip on the control matrix. Instead of directing each gargoyle's actions, I provided structural support while allowing Dylan's chaos magic to find natural patterns within the pandemonium.

The effect was immediate and startling.

The gargoyles stopped fighting our control and began... improvising. The conflicting musical styles merged into something that was part opera, part jazz, part entirely new form of artistic expression. The acrobatic stunts became dance moves that complemented the musical performance. The magical chaos transformed into collaborative creativity.

It was beautiful. It was impossible. It was everything partnership magic was supposed to be.

But it was also draining our magical reserves at an alarming rate.

"Dylan," I said through gritted teeth, "we can't maintain this much longer."

"I know. But look at them, Lyra. Look what we created."

I looked. The gargoyles were performing something that had never existed before—a fusion of individual artistry and collaborative magic that spoke to everything we'd discovered about partnership bonds. Students were emerging from buildings across campus, drawn by the impossible music. Faculty members stood in doorways, their expressions ranging from amazement to concern.

And there, in the crowd gathered below, I spotted Professor Arcturus himself, his pale face turned upward toward our demonstration.

"He's watching," I said.

"Good. Let him see what partnership magic really looks like."

But our magical reserves were nearly exhausted, and I could feel the partnership bond beginning to fray under the sustained pressure.

I could feel it slipping—like trying to hold water in my hands. Panic clawed at me. If we didn't stop now, we wouldn't just lose control of the spell—we might lose each other.

"Dylan, we have to end this. Now."

"One more minute—"

"Now!"

Together, we began the shutdown sequence, carefully reducing magical flow to each gargoyle while maintaining enough connection to ensure they returned to their pedestals safely rather than simply collapsing.

The first five gargoyles settled into dormancy smoothly. The sixth—the one that had caused the initial conflict—fought the shutdown, its magical signature still clashing with our bond.

And that's when it all unraveled.

The feedback loop from the resistant gargoyle interacted with our exhausted magical reserves in exactly the way I'd been afraid it might. Our partnership bond didn't just fluctuate—it destabilized completely, sending both of us reeling as months of carefully built magical connection shattered.

The last thing I remembered was Dylan's hand in mine, our magic tearing apart like fabric under too much strain, and the sickening sensation of falling into magical emptiness where our bond had been.

Then darkness claimed me, and I knew nothing more.

———

I woke up in the Medical Wing, surrounded by sterile white walls and gentle healing magic. Pale sunlight slanted across the room, suggesting I'd been unconscious for hours.

"Lyra?" Dylan's voice, hoarse and worried, came from somewhere to my right.

I turned my head—carefully, because everything felt fragile and strange—to find him sitting in a chair beside my bed. He looked terrible: pale, exhausted, with dark circles under his eyes that spoke to a sleepless night.

"Hey," I said softly, my voice coming out rougher than expected.

"Hey." His smile was weak but genuine. "How are you feeling?"

I took inventory. Physically, I seemed to be intact, though there was a bone-deep exhaustion that suggested magical depletion. Emotionally, I felt... hollow. Like something important was missing.

And then I realized what it was.

"Dylan," I said carefully, "try to reach for our partnership bond."

His expression went very still. "Lyra—"

"Try."

I watched his face as he closed his eyes and reached for the magical connection that had become as natural as breathing. Watched as hope turned to confusion, confusion to growing alarm.

"I can't feel it," he said quietly. "I can't feel you at all."

The words confirmed what I'd already suspected but hoped wasn't true.

Our partnership bond was gone.

Months of magical development, emotional connection, and revolutionary discovery—destroyed in a single night by our own ambition and a gargoyle with an incompatible magical signature.

"Lyra," Dylan said desperately, "tell me this is temporary. Tell me magical bonds can recover from this kind of damage."

I wanted to reassure him. Wanted to say that partnership

magic was resilient, that what we'd built together could be rebuilt.

Instead, I found myself remembering Professor Lumina's warnings about the dangers of magical overextension and the historical cases of bonded pairs who'd never recovered from traumatic separations.

"I don't know," I whispered. The absence inside me was deafening. For weeks, Dylan's magic had been a song beside mine. Now, there was only silence. Hollow, cold silence. "Dylan, I honestly don't know."

The silence that followed was filled with everything we might have lost forever.

CHAPTER FOURTEEN
WINTER BREAK

DYLAN

The Vixen family estate looked exactly the same as it had when I'd left for sophomore year three months ago—sprawling stone manor covered in perpetual frost, ancient oak trees whose bare branches sparkled with ice crystals, and the familiar scent of pine smoke drifting from multiple chimneys. It should have felt like coming home.

Instead, standing in the circular driveway with my luggage at my feet, I felt like an impostor wearing my own skin.

"Dylan!" My mother's voice carried across the courtyard, warm with genuine delight. She emerged from the main entrance in a swirl of emerald robes, her auburn hair catching the winter light. "You're early! We weren't expecting you until this evening."

"Classes ended sooner than planned," I said, accepting her embrace and trying to muster enthusiasm I didn't feel. "Magical mishap in the final demonstration. They sent everyone home early for safety evaluations."

It wasn't technically a lie. There had been a magical mishap, and the administration was conducting safety evaluations—specifically of partnership magic research and the students who'd been involved in studying it. What I didn't mention was that the "magical mishap" had destroyed the most important thing that had ever happened to me.

"Well, we're thrilled to have you home," Mom said, linking her arm through mine as we walked toward the house. "Your father's in his study going over the quarterly reports, and your brothers should be arriving tomorrow. It'll be wonderful to have the whole family together again."

"Yeah," I agreed hollowly. "Wonderful."

The Vixen estate's interior was a testament to centuries of successful fox shifter magic—enchanted portraits that nodded in greeting, self-organizing libraries, and warming charms that adjusted themselves based on individual preference. Everything was elegant, efficient, and comfortable in the way that old money and older magic could provide.

I'd grown up surrounded by this kind of casual luxury, and until recently, I'd taken it for granted. Now, after months of partnership magic and revolutionary discoveries, the pristine perfection felt stifling.

"How was the semester, dear?" Mom asked as we settled into the sitting room, where house sprites had already arranged tea and cakes. "Your last letters were a bit... sparse on details."

That was because the details had involved falling in love with a brilliant light mage, discovering that my supposedly defective magic was actually evolutionary, and accidentally destroying our magical bond in a spectacular public demonstration that had probably ended both our academic careers.

"It was educational," I said carefully.

"I'm sure it was." Mom's green eyes—so similar to my own—studied my face with the kind of maternal intuition that missed nothing. "Dylan, you look tired. And thin. Have you been eating properly?"

"Campus food, you know how it is."

"Hmm." She didn't look convinced. "Well, we'll fix that while you're home. Mrs McCreedy's already planning your favorite meals."

I nodded and smiled and made appropriate responses to her questions about professors and classes, and social activities. But part of my mind kept drifting to a sterile medical wing where I'd sat beside Lyra's bed, watching her process the loss of our magical connection with the same analytical detachment she brought to failed experiments.

We should give each other space, she'd said in that carefully controlled voice. *Time to process what's happened without the complication of proximity.*

Space had turned out to be academic code for *maybe it's better if we don't see each other over winter break.*

"Dylan?" Mom's voice pulled me back to the present. "I asked about your plans for the holiday."

"Sorry, just thinking. No specific plans. Rest, family time, maybe some reading."

"Reading?" Mom's eyebrows rose with surprise. "Voluntary reading? During vacation?"

Before this semester, the idea of spending break with books would have horrified me. Now, the thought of diving into magical theory texts—trying to find some reference to partnership bond repair, some hope that what we'd lost could be recovered—felt like the only productive use of my time.

"I've developed an interest in advanced magical theory," I said.

"How wonderfully academic of you." Mom's smile was

pleased but puzzled. "Though I have to say, this newfound scholarly inclination is rather unexpected."

"People change."

"They do indeed." She reached over to squeeze my hand. "I'm proud of you, you know. Whatever's prompted this growth, it suits you."

The warmth in her voice made my chest ache. How could I explain that the person she was proud of—the Dylan who'd discovered intellectual passion and academic purpose—might not exist anymore? That the magical partnership that had made me feel brilliant and capable and worthy was gone, leaving behind only the mediocre student I'd always been?

"Thanks, Mom."

"Now," she said, settling back with her tea, "tell me about this girl."

I nearly choked on my cake. "What girl?"

"The one responsible for this dramatic personality transformation." Mom's smile turned knowing. "Dylan, I've raised three sons. I recognize the signs of romantic attachment."

"I don't know what you're talking about."

"The faraway looks, the distraction, the sudden interest in academic pursuits, the fact that you've written exactly three letters home this semester and none of them mentioned any social activities." She ticked off the evidence on her fingers. "Either you've fallen in love, or you've developed a serious magical research obsession."

Both, I thought miserably. *And I've lost them both.*

"Her name is Lyra," I said quietly.

"And?"

"And it's complicated."

Mom waited with the patient expectation of someone who'd spent decades extracting information from evasive fox shifters.

"She's brilliant," I continued reluctantly. "The smartest person I've ever met. We were... we had a research partnership. Magical theory work."

"Had?"

"The project ended badly." I stared into my teacup, watching steam curl in patterns that reminded me of the light constructs Lyra and I used to create together. "There was an accident. Now she thinks it's better if we maintain some distance while we figure out what comes next."

"Ah." Mom's expression softened with understanding. "Your first heartbreak."

"It's not—" I started, then stopped. Because it was, wasn't it? The loss of our magical partnership was devastating, but the loss of Lyra herself was worse. The thought that she might decide we were better off apart, that the Dylan without revolutionary magic wasn't worth her time, felt like a weight sitting on my chest.

"Oh, sweetheart," Mom said gently, moving to sit beside me on the couch. "I'm sorry."

"The worst part," I said, surprised to hear myself talking, "is that she was right about the distance. Being around each other right now is... difficult. Everything reminds us of what we lost."

"What did you lose, exactly?"

How could I explain magical partnership to someone who'd never experienced it? How could I describe the way Lyra's magic had felt like a missing piece of myself, or the harmony we'd achieved when our abilities worked together?

"A connection," I said finally. "Something that made both of us better than we were alone."

"And you think it can't be rebuilt?"

"I don't know. Maybe. But what if it can't? What if we've lost it forever, and Lyra realizes she's better off without me dragging down her academic career?"

Mom was quiet for a moment, considering.

"Dylan," she said finally, "may I tell you something about your father and me?"

I nodded.

"When we first met, I was convinced we were completely incompatible. He was chaos incarnate—spontaneous, disorganized, always three steps ahead of disaster. I was structure and planning, and careful consideration of consequences."

"That sounds familiar," I said with a weak smile.

"We had a spectacular fight during our third year of university. Something about a prank gone wrong and conflicting approaches to magical problem-solving. I told him we were too different to work together, that his chaotic approach would always clash with my methodical nature."

"What happened?"

"We spent six miserable weeks avoiding each other while I tried to convince myself I was better off alone." Mom's smile turned wry. "Turns out, chaos and structure aren't opposing forces. They're complementary ones. He taught me to embrace spontaneity; I taught him the value of planning. Together, we became something neither of us could have achieved individually."

"But what if the connection is gone? What if we can't get back what we had?"

"Then you build something new." Mom reached over to tuck a strand of hair behind my ear, the gesture achingly familiar from childhood. "Love isn't about recapturing perfect moments, Dylan. It's about choosing to grow together despite imperfection."

"Even if we've both changed? Even if I'm not the person she fell for anymore?"

"Especially then." Mom's voice was warm with conviction.

"The best partnerships aren't built on who you were when you met. They're built on who you choose to become together."

I wanted to believe her. Wanted to think that maybe Lyra and I could find our way back to each other, even without the magical partnership that had brought us together. But the memory of her carefully distant expression in the medical wing, the way she'd pulled back when I'd tried to take her hand, suggested otherwise.

"What if she's moved on?" I asked quietly. "What if she's decided she's better off without me?"

"Then you fight for her," Mom said simply. "You show her that what you have together is worth fighting for, magical partnership or no magical partnership."

"How?"

"By being the person she fell in love with. By proving that you didn't just care about the magic—you cared about her."

I thought about that as the afternoon wore on, as Dad emerged from his study to welcome me home with backslapping affection, as the house filled with the familiar sounds and smells of a Vixen family gathering. My parents clearly expected me to settle back into the comfortable rhythms of home life, but I felt disconnected from it all.

The Dylan who'd left for NPU had been content to drift through life on charm and inherited privilege. The Dylan who'd returned had tasted what it felt like to be truly brilliant, truly powerful, truly necessary to someone else's happiness.

I wasn't sure which version of myself I was supposed to be anymore.

That evening, I found myself in the estate's library, surrounded by dusty tomes on magical theory that I'd never paid attention to before. Most were focused on individual casting techniques and traditional magical education—nothing that would help with partnership bond restoration.

But buried in a section on historical magical practices, I found something that made me sit up with sudden interest.

"Partnership Bonds: Recovery and Restoration" by Master Elias Thornfield, dated 1847.

The book was old, its leather binding cracked with age, but the magical preservation charms had kept the pages readable. I opened it carefully, heart racing with the first hope I'd felt in days.

"The common misconception about magical partnerships," the introduction read, *"is that the bond itself is the source of power. In truth, the bond is merely a manifestation of deeper compatibility— emotional, intellectual, and spiritual alignment that exists independently of magical connection. While traumatic separation can indeed sever the magical aspects of partnership, the underlying compatibility remains intact, waiting to be rediscovered through conscious effort and renewed trust."*

I read the passage three times, hardly daring to believe what it suggested.

If Thornfield was right, then what Lyra and I had lost wasn't really gone—it was dormant. Waiting for us to find our way back to the emotional and intellectual connection that had made the magical partnership possible in the first place.

"The key to restoration," I read on, *"lies not in attempting to recreate the original bond, but in building a new foundation based on deeper understanding and conscious choice rather than magical accident."*

For the first time since waking up in the medical wing, I felt something that might have been hope.

Maybe the magical partnership was gone forever. Maybe we could never recreate the exact harmony we'd achieved during our first discoveries. But maybe that didn't matter.

Maybe what mattered was proving to Lyra that I'd fallen in love with her, not just with our magical compatibility. That I valued her brilliance, her courage, her stubborn determination to fight for what she believed in—not because these qualities enhanced my magic, but because they enhanced my life.

Maybe Mom was right. Maybe the best partnerships weren't about recapturing perfect moments, but about choosing to grow together despite imperfection.

And maybe, just maybe, Lyra was spending her winter break coming to the same conclusion.

I spent the rest of the evening reading Thornfield's work, taking careful notes and formulating a plan that had nothing to do with magic and everything to do with the girl who'd taught me what it meant to be brilliant.

By the time I went to bed, I knew exactly what I needed to do when I returned to NPU.

The question was whether I'd have the courage to do it.

———

THE NEXT MORNING brought my brothers home in a whirlwind of luggage, laughter, and competitive storytelling. Marcus and Adrian were both older, both successful in their respective magical careers, and both delighted to have their baby brother home for the holidays.

"Dylan!" Marcus swept me into a bear hug that lifted me off my feet. "Look at you, all scholarly and serious. What happened to the kid who used to put itching powder in my formal robes?"

"He grew up," I said, extricating myself from his embrace.

"Tragic," Adrian said with mock solemnity. "Another promising prankster lost to academic responsibility."

They were teasing, but there was genuine affection underneath it. My brothers had always been protective of me, the youngest and least academically successful of the three Vixen sons. Growing up, they'd covered for my magical mishaps, helped with homework I couldn't manage alone, and never made me feel inadequate despite their obvious superiority in everything magical.

Now, sitting around the breakfast table listening to their stories of professional success and romantic adventures, I realized something had shifted. I no longer felt like the disappointing younger brother who needed protection and assistance.

I felt like someone who'd discovered his own worth and was ready to fight for what mattered to him.

"So," Adrian said around a mouthful of enchanted pancakes, "Mom mentioned there's a girl involved in this personality transformation."

"There is," I said simply.

"And?" Marcus prompted.

"And I'm going to win her back."

My brothers exchanged glances.

"Win her back?" Adrian's eyebrows rose. "What did you do wrong?"

"I didn't do anything wrong. We both made choices that seemed logical at the time but turned out to be mistakes."

"Such as?"

I found myself explaining the partnership magic research, the faculty opposition, the spectacular demonstration, and the devastating aftermath. Not the technical details—those would have required more magical theory background than either of my brothers possessed—but the emotional core of what we'd discovered and lost.

"So you fell in love with a brilliant academic who helped you discover abilities you never knew you had," Marcus summarized when I finished.

"Yes."

"And then you lost both the abilities and the girl in a dramatic, magical accident," Adrian added.

"Yes."

"And now you want to prove that you didn't just love her magic, you loved her," Marcus continued.

"Exactly."

My brothers looked at each other again, then back at me.

"What's your plan?" Adrian asked.

For the first time in days, I smiled. "I'm going to build her a light garden."

"A what now?"

"A garden made entirely of sustained light magic. Every flower, every tree, every blade of grass crafted from pure luminous energy and maintained indefinitely without partnership bond assistance."

"Dylan," Marcus said carefully, "you realize that kind of advanced light magic is typically beyond individual casting ability? Especially for fox shifters?"

"I know."

"And you're planning to attempt it anyway?"

"I'm planning to master it," I corrected. "Because Lyra taught me that magic isn't about what you're supposedly good at. It's about what you're willing to work for."

"And if you can't manage it?" Adrian asked gently.

"Then I'll find another way to show her what she means to me." I looked at my brothers, these two successful, confident men who'd always seemed impossibly capable to my younger self. "But I'm going to try. Because she's worth trying for."

Marcus grinned suddenly. "Well, damn. Look who finally figured out what he wants."

"About time," Adrian agreed. "So, little brother, how can we help?"

The offer was unexpected and overwhelmingly generous.

"You want to help?"

"Dylan," Marcus said seriously, "we've been watching you drift through life for years, charming your way through challenges without ever really caring about the outcome. This is the first time you've talked about something that actually matters to you."

"The first time you've sounded like you know who you want to be," Adrian added.

"Of course we're going to help."

And that's how I ended up spending the remainder of winter break in intensive magical training with my brothers, working to master light magic techniques that should have been impossible for a fox shifter attempting them alone.

It was exhausting, frustrating work. Without Lyra's structural framework to guide my chaotic energy, every spell required exponentially more effort and concentration. Progress was measured in tiny increments rather than breakthrough moments.

But slowly, gradually, I began to understand what Lyra had tried to teach me about discipline and a systematic approach. I learned to channel my natural magical instincts through careful theoretical preparation. I discovered that individual magical achievement wasn't about raw power—it was about patience, precision, and the willingness to fail repeatedly until you succeeded.

By the time winter break ended, I could maintain complex light constructs for nearly an hour without assistance. It wasn't partnership magic—it didn't have the effortless harmony or exponential enhancement that came from magical collaboration.

But it was mine. Individual achievement earned through dedicated effort, guided by everything Lyra had taught me about approaching magic with intellectual rigor.

It was proof that I'd internalized her lessons even without our bond.

And maybe, just maybe, it would be enough to convince her that what we'd built together was worth rebuilding in whatever form it could take.

The question was whether she'd give me the chance to try.

As the sleigh carried me back to NPU for the spring semester, I clutched Thornfield's book in one hand and a small crystal containing the first light flower I'd successfully created alone in the other.

Time to find out if the partnership could survive the loss of partnership magic.

Time to discover whether love was stronger than the fear of imperfection.

CHAPTER FIFTEEN

REPAIR AND REBUILD

LYRA

I was alone in the Observatory when Dylan returned to campus, three days before spring semester officially began. The early arrival shouldn't have surprised me—punctuality had become one of his unexpected traits over the course of our partnership—but it did catch me off guard.

I'd been spending most of winter break in the Observatory despite officially having no access to research facilities. Professor Lumina had quietly arranged for my keycard to continue working, though we both pretended this was an oversight rather than a deliberate kindness. The alternative—spending weeks at home with my parents' pointed questions about my academic future—had seemed infinitely worse than haunting the empty campus like some kind of scholarly ghost.

I told myself I was here for the research. That rebuilding from memory was an academic necessity, not an emotional crutch. But each time I reached for an answer we'd once found together, all I touched was absence.

The soft chime of the Observatory door made me look up from the theoretical framework I'd been rebuilding from memory. Dylan stood in the entrance, looking simultaneously nervous and determined, with a travel bag slung over his shoulder and what appeared to be a large, ornate box floating behind him.

"Hi," he said simply.

"Hi yourself." I saved my work with a gesture, pretending the skip in my chest was surprise, not hope. "You're early."

"So are you."

"I never left."

Something flickered across his expression—concern, maybe, or guilt. "Lyra, you spent the entire break here? Alone?"

"Not entirely alone. Professor Lumina checked on me regularly. And the maintenance sprites are surprisingly good conversationalists."

It was a weak attempt at humor, but Dylan's worried frown suggested it hadn't been convincing.

"That's..." He paused, seeming to choose his words carefully. "That must have been lonely."

"I'm used to solitude," I said, which was true but sounded harsher than I'd intended.

"Are you? Because I remember someone who used to light up the Observatory just by having a partner to share her discoveries with."

His words struck like light through glass—clarifying and painful. I turned back to my work displays, hoping he couldn't see the way my hands had started to tremble slightly.

"That was different," I said quietly. "That was when we had the magical partnership. When the research mattered to someone besides just me."

"It still matters to me."

"Dylan—"

"I know we can't recreate what we had," he interrupted, moving further into the Observatory with that careful precision he'd developed during our sessions together. "I know the magical partnership might be gone forever. But that doesn't mean the work we did together was worthless."

I finally turned to face him, and was struck by how different he looked. Not physically—he was still the same attractive fox shifter with rust-colored hair and green eyes that seemed to see straight through to my soul. But there was something in his posture, his expression, that spoke to confidence earned rather than inherited.

The boy who once coasted on charm now stood before me as a man shaped by purpose.

"Lyra, I know we agreed to give each other space. I know we said we'd figure out what comes next without the complication of proximity. But I can't just pretend that what we had meant nothing."

"I never said I didn't feel the loss in my bones—"

"You said it was better if we maintained distance," Dylan interrupted gently. "You said being around each other was difficult because everything reminded us of what we'd lost."

The words were accurate, and they stung because I'd meant them when I said them. The first few days after losing our magical connection had been agony—every shared glance, every casual touch, every moment of trying to reach for the harmony that was no longer there had felt like pressing on a fresh wound.

But the weeks of solitude that followed had been worse.

"Dylan," I said carefully, "the magical partnership was extraordinary. What we achieved together, the way our abilities enhanced each other—that was something unprecedented in modern magical education."

"I know."

"And without it, we're just..." I struggled to find words that wouldn't sound cruel. "We're just two students who used to work well together."

"Are we?" Dylan moved to my central platform, his hand hovering over the controls, eyes searching mine for permission—as if he wasn't sure he had the right to light up my world again. "Because I'd like to show you something."

The Observatory filled with light—not the combined radiance of our partnership magic, but something entirely different. Individual light constructs of breathtaking complexity began materializing around us, each one crafted with precision that spoke to months of painstaking practice.

Flowers bloomed from nothing—each one a declaration, a question, an apology—their petals catching and refracting Aurora patterns. Trees grew from the platform floor, their branches spreading to create a canopy of pure luminescence. Grass carpeted the space around our feet, each blade individually crafted and maintained.

It was a garden made entirely of light magic. A garden that existed independently of partnership bonds or magical collaboration.

"Dylan," I breathed, turning in a slow circle to take in the scope of what he'd created. "This is impossible. Light magic of this complexity, sustained without external support—"

"Is exactly what you taught me magic could be if I was willing to work for it," he finished. "Lyra, you showed me that magical ability isn't about what you're supposedly good at. It's about what you're willing to learn."

I reached out to touch one of the luminous flowers, marveling at its solidity and warmth. "You did this alone? Without any partnership enhancement?"

"Completely alone. Using everything you taught me about a

systematic approach and theoretical preparation." Dylan's voice carried quiet pride. "It took me three weeks to create a single flower that lasted more than five minutes. But I kept working at it because I wanted to prove something."

"What?"

"That I didn't fall in love with our magical partnership." He moved closer, his green eyes serious and vulnerable. "I fell in love with the person who made me want to be better than I was. Who saw potential in me that I'd never recognized. Who fought the entire NPU administration to defend what we'd discovered together."

My breath caught. "Dylan—"

"I fell in love with you, Lyra. Not with what your magic could do for mine, but with your brilliance, your courage, your stubborn determination to ask questions that didn't have comfortable answers." The light garden pulsed around us, responding to his emotional state. "And if our magical partnership is gone forever, if we can never recreate that perfect harmony we used to achieve— I'm okay with that. Because what I want isn't a magical collaboration. It's you."

The words hung in the air between us, loaded with hope and fear and the weight of everything we'd lost and found and might lose again.

"You spent your entire winter break learning advanced light magic," I said slowly, "to prove that you loved me rather than our partnership."

"Among other things, yes."

"That's..." I looked around at the impossible garden he'd created through sheer determination and individual skill. "That's either the most romantic gesture in NPU history or the most elaborate academic demonstration ever attempted."

"Can't it be both?"

Despite everything—the lost partnership, the uncertainty about our future, the fear that we might never recapture what we'd had—I found myself smiling.

"You know," I said thoughtfully, "there's something beautifully symmetrical about a fox shifter mastering light magic to win back a light mage who taught him systematic magical theory."

"Is that what I'm doing? Winning you back?"

The careful hope in his voice made my chest ache. Because the truth was, he'd never really lost me. The magical partnership might be gone, but the connection beneath it—the intellectual compatibility, the emotional understanding, the way he made me feel like the best version of myself—that had never wavered.

"Dylan," I said softly, "you never needed to win me back. You needed to convince me that we could build something new together. Something that didn't depend on a magical partnership to exist."

"And?"

I gestured to the light garden surrounding us, at the reconstructed research crystals on my platform, at the evidence of months of dedicated work undertaken not for personal gain but to repair what he thought we'd lost.

"I think you may have just succeeded."

Dylan's answering smile was radiant enough to power the entire Observatory.

"So what happens now?" he asked.

"Now," I said, moving closer until I could take his hands without the stabbing pain of missing magical connection, "we figure out what partnership looks like when it's built on choice rather than magical accident."

The moment our skin touched, something extraordinary happened. Not the return of our original bond—that harmony was gone, probably forever—but something new. Something that felt like recognition, like coming home, like two people choosing to build something together because they wanted to rather than because magic had decided for them.

"It feels different," Dylan said quietly.

"Better or worse?"

"Different," he repeated thoughtfully. "More... intentional. Like we're here because we choose to be, not because our magic chose for us."

I understood what he meant. The original partnership bond had been magical serendipity—a perfect confluence of compatible abilities that had created something neither of us could have achieved alone. This felt more grounded, more deliberate. Less magic, more choice.

"I missed you," I admitted. "These past weeks, working alone in the Observatory—I kept turning to share discoveries with someone who wasn't there."

"I missed you too. Which is how I knew that what we had was more than just magical compatibility."

"What was it, then?"

Dylan's smile was soft and sure. "Partnership. Real partnership. The kind that survives imperfection and grows stronger because of conscious choice rather than magical accident."

As we stood there in his impossible light garden, hands intertwined and the Observatory glowing around us with evidence of dedication and determination, and love expressed through academic achievement, I realized that losing our magical bond might have been the best thing that could have happened to us.

Because now we knew, beyond any doubt, that what we'd built together was strong enough to survive anything.

Even the loss of magic itself.

"So," I said, looking around at the luminous garden that

would have been impossible for either of us to create six months ago, "what should we work on next?"

"Together?"

"Always together."

Dylan's grin was pure fox shifter mischief. "Well, I did have some ideas about advanced partnership theory that don't require magical bonds..."

"Academic partnership theory?"

"Among other kinds."

And as we began planning our next collaboration—magical, intellectual, and romantic—I couldn't help but think that some-times the most important discoveries happened not when every-thing went according to plan, but when you were brave enough to rebuild from the ground up.

Sometimes the most powerful magic was simply choosing, again and again, to stand beside someone who made you want to be the best version of yourself.

Because real partnership wasn't something magic gave us. It was something we chose to create—again and again—with open hands and open hearts.

CHAPTER SIXTEEN

FIRST KISS IN THE OBSERVATORY

DYLAN

Working with Lyra again felt like rediscovering a language I'd forgotten I knew how to speak.

We'd spent the past three days rebuilding not just our academic partnership, but the easy rhythm of collaboration that had made our original magical bond so powerful. Without the overwhelming harmony of shared magical energy, I could actually appreciate the subtler ways we complemented each other—how Lyra's systematic approach gave structure to my creative leaps, how my willingness to embrace chaos helped her push beyond safe theoretical boundaries.

It was a partnership without the partnership magic. And somehow, it felt more intentional, more precious, because we were choosing it rather than being swept along by magical compatibility.

There was no hum of bond-magic guiding us now—just two separate forces learning to coexist again. And yet, something shimmered beneath the surface, unspoken and waiting.

"Dylan, could you check the resonance calculations on the aurora projection spell?" Lyra called from where she was fine-tuning the Observatory's main display system. "I want to make sure we're not accidentally creating another campus-wide light show."

"Right, because the last time we did that, it worked out so well for us," I said dryly, pulling up the mathematical frameworks she'd asked me to review.

We were preparing for tomorrow's presentation to the Academic Review Board—Lyra's final chance to prove that her research deserved reinstatement, and our mutual opportunity to demonstrate that partnership magic theory could produce practical applications without dangerous instability.

"The calculations look solid," I reported, running through the energy distribution patterns one more time. "Maximum visual impact, minimal risk of systemic magical overflow."

"Good." Lyra made a few final adjustments to the projection matrix, then stepped back to survey our work. "I think we're ready."

The Observatory looked like a magical laboratory crossed with an art installation. Floating displays showed theoretical frameworks for controlled aurora generation, while carefully positioned light crystals created focusing arrays that would channel our combined magical energy into precise patterns rather than chaotic displays.

It was elegant, sophisticated, and exactly the kind of controlled demonstration that would convince the Review Board that partnership magic could be academically responsible.

"Nervous?" I asked, moving to stand beside her at the central platform.

"Terrified," Lyra admitted with a rueful smile. "If this doesn't work, if we can't prove that partnership theory has practical applications..."

"Then we'll figure out something else," I said firmly. "Lyra, whether or not the Review Board reinstates your research privileges, whether or not they decide partnership magic is academically acceptable—that doesn't change what we've accomplished together."

"Doesn't it?" She turned to face me, and I could see the fear she'd been trying to hide behind academic preparation. "Dylan, what if they're right? What if partnership magic is inherently unstable, inherently dangerous? What if we've been pursuing something that's more likely to hurt people than help them?"

The vulnerability in her voice made my chest ache. This was the fear that had been eating at her since our bond shattered—not just that we'd lost our magical connection, but that maybe we'd been wrong to pursue it in the first place.

"Do you remember," I said carefully, "the first time we successfully created light constructs together? In this room, with your theoretical frameworks guiding my chaos magic?"

"Of course."

"And how did that feel?"

Lyra was quiet for a moment, remembering. "Like magic the way it was supposed to be. Like discovering that everything I'd been trying to achieve alone was just the beginning of what was possible."

"That feeling—that sense of rightness, of potential, of magic expanding beyond individual limitations—do you think that was dangerous?"

"No, but—"

"Do you think the gargoyle opera was dangerous? Even when it went wrong?"

"Dylan, we lost our magical bond. How is that not dangerous?"

"Because we're still here," I said simply. "Still working together, still discovering new applications for partnership theory, still proving that magical collaboration can create beauty instead of chaos. We lost the magical connection, yes. But we didn't lose what made that connection possible in the first place."

I gestured to the Observatory around us, at the evidence of weeks of collaborative work.

"Lyra, look what we've built together without magical partnership enhancement. Look at the research we've developed, the theoretical frameworks we've expanded, and the practical applications we've designed. If this isn't proof that partnership magic theory has value, then I don't know what would be."

"But what if the Review Board doesn't see it that way? What if they decide that any risk of magical bond disruption makes the entire field too dangerous to pursue?"

The fear in her voice was raw, real, and completely understandable. Lyra had built her entire academic identity around magical research, and the thought of having that taken away—especially for defending something she believed in—had to be terrifying.

"Then we'll know we fought for something worth fighting for," I said, reaching for her hands. "And we'll figure out what comes next."

The moment our skin touched, something extraordinary happened.

Not the return of our original magical bond—that harmony was gone forever. But something new, something that felt like recognition on a level deeper than magic. Like two people who'd found their way back to each other not because of external forces, but because of deliberate choice.

"Dylan," Lyra said softly, her pale eyes searching my face. "What if we can't recreate what we had? What if this is as close as we ever get to that perfect magical harmony?"

"Then this is enough," I said without hesitation. "Lyra, that magical bond was incredible, but it was never the most important thing about us working together."

"What was?"

"The fact that you make me want to be better than I am. The way you see potential in me that I never recognized myself. The fact that being around you makes me feel like the smartest, most capable version of myself."

I moved closer, until we were standing close enough that I could see the flecks of silver in her blue eyes.

"And maybe," I continued, my voice dropping to something just above a whisper, "the fact that I'm completely, desperately in love with you."

Lyra's breath caught. "Dylan—"

"I know we agreed to rebuild slowly. I know we said we'd figure out what partnership looks like without magical enhancement. But Lyra, I can't spend another day pretending that what I feel for you is purely academic."

"Who said anything about purely academic?" she asked, her voice soft and wondering.

"I—what?"

"Dylan, did you really think I spent three days working sixteen-hour days with you because I was interested in the research applications?"

I blinked. "Weren't you?"

"I was interested in the research applications," Lyra said with a smile that was part amusement, part affection, and entirely devastating. "But mostly, I was interested in the researcher."

"The researcher?"

"The brilliant, stubborn, impossibly sweet fox shifter who spent his entire winter break recreating months of my work because he thought I needed it back." She stepped closer, until there was barely any space left between us. "The man who mastered advanced light magic through sheer determination because he wanted to prove that what we had together was worth more than magical convenience."

"Lyra—"

"I love you too, Dylan Vixen. Irreversibly," she said simply. "I love your creativity, your willingness to embrace chaos and find beauty in it. I love the way you make me laugh, the way you challenge my assumptions, the way you make everything feel possible."

"Even without magical partnership?"

"Especially without magical partnership." Her smile was radiant. "Because now I know for certain that what we have together isn't dependent on magic. It's just... us."

The word hung in the air between us, loaded with promise and possibility and the weight of everything we'd discovered and lost and chosen to rebuild.

"Us," I repeated, marveling at how much hope could fit into two simple letters.

"Us," Lyra confirmed. "Dylan, would you—"

But I was already moving, closing the last few inches between us to cup her face in my hands. I'd imagined this moment a hundred times since Winter break—but standing here, watching her look at me like I mattered beyond magic, I realized I was terrified. Not of rejection. Of everything this meant.

"Can I kiss you?"

"I've been waiting since you got back."

And with that one comment, I kissed her.

I wanted it to be soft, a kiss that acknowledged everything

we'd been through and everything we hoped to rebuild together. Instead, it was alchemy—choice transmuted into power.

Not the overwhelming harmony of our lost partnership bond, but something deeper, more fundamental. The magic of two people choosing each other completely, of an emotional connection that transcended any external enhancement.

The moment our lips touched, the Observatory responded.

Light bloomed around us—not from any spell we'd cast, but from the intersection of our individual magical signatures. This wasn't magic forcing us into harmony—it was our magic answering the harmony we'd built ourselves. Where my chaotic energy met her structured precision, aurora patterns began painting themselves across the dome overhead. The carefully positioned light crystals we'd arranged for tomorrow's demonstration activated spontaneously, creating cascading displays of silver and gold radiance.

But this time, instead of the dangerous magical overload that had destroyed our bond, the energy felt controlled, beautiful, sustainable like our individual magics had learned to dance together without losing their distinct qualities.

When we finally broke apart, the entire Observatory was filled with gentle, swirling lights that pulsed in rhythm with our heartbeats.

"Did we just—" Lyra began.

"Manifest magic from a kiss?" I finished, looking around at the impossible beauty surrounding us. "I think we did."

"Without trying. Without any formal spell structure or theoretical framework."

"Just from kissing each other," I added with wonder.

Lyra laughed, the sound bright and incredulous. "Dylan, do you realize what this means?"

"That we're even more magically compatible than we origi-nally thought?"

"That we've discovered a new form of partnership magic." Her eyes were bright with excitement and discovery. "Not the depen-dent, bonded connection we had before, but something collabora-tive and voluntary. Magic that responds to emotional connection rather than formal magical partnership."

I looked around at the aurora patterns still dancing overhead, at the evidence of magic created through choice rather than accident.

"So we've accidentally discovered the holy grail of partnership magic theory," I said. "Collaborative magical enhancement without the risks of formal bonding."

"While kissing in my Observatory," Lyra added with a grin. "I have to say, this is not how I expected our research to progress."

"Disappointed?"

"Are you kidding?" She gestured to the lights still swirling around us. "Dylan, this is exactly the kind of practical application that the Review Board needs to see. Proof that partnership magic can be both powerful and stable, both collaborative and inde-pendent."

"So tomorrow's presentation just became significantly more interesting."

"Tomorrow's presentation just became a demonstration that could revolutionize magical education theory." Lyra's smile was brilliant. "Though I suppose we should probably test the repro-ducibility of this effect."

"Test the reproducibility?"

"You know, make sure this wasn't just a one-time occurrence." Her expression was innocently academic, but there was mischief dancing in her eyes. "Rigorous scientific method requires multiple data points."

"Lyra Lumina," I said with delight, "are you suggesting we need to kiss again for research purposes?"

"I'm suggesting," she said, moving closer until her hands rested against my chest, "that a thorough investigation of this phenomenon is crucial to our academic understanding."

"Well," I said, pulling her closer, "far be it from me to interfere with rigorous scientific methodology."

The second kiss was even better than the first. Partly because we weren't surprised by the magical response this time, partly because we could focus on each other rather than worrying about what it meant.

But mostly because it felt like coming home to someone who'd been waiting for me my entire life.

The aurora displays that bloomed around our kiss were more complex, more beautiful, more perfectly coordinated than anything we'd achieved during our original magical partnership. They painted the Observatory in patterns that spoke to harmony without dependency, collaboration without loss of individual identity.

When we finally came up for air, I realized that everything had changed.

Not just our magical understanding, not just our research prospects, but us. The careful distance we'd maintained since losing our bond was gone, replaced by something that felt solid, certain, and completely unafraid of whatever challenges might come.

"So," I said, my arms still wrapped around her, aurora light dancing in her dark hair, "what happens now?"

"Now," Lyra said with a smile that was part joy, part determination, and entirely unstoppable, "we show the Academic Review Board exactly what partnership magic can accomplish when it's built on choice rather than accident."

"And after that?"

"After that, we figure out what comes next. Together."

"Always together?"

"Always together," she confirmed, standing on her toes to press a soft kiss to my lips. "Though I should probably warn you, I have some ideas about collaborative research projects that might keep us busy for the next few decades."

"Academic projects?"

"Among other kinds."

As I looked around at the impossible beauty we'd created simply by choosing each other, at the evidence of magic that responded to love rather than formal partnership, I couldn't help but think that the next few decades were going to be very interesting indeed.

Because we'd discovered something that no amount of institutional opposition could take away from us: that the most powerful magic wasn't something you found by accident.

It was something you built, day by day, choice by choice, heartbeat by heartbeat, kiss by kiss, with someone who made you believe that anything was possible.

And tomorrow, we were going to prove it to the world.

CHAPTER SEVENTEEN
THE HEIST DEEPENS

LYRA

The emergency alarm that woke me at three in the morning wasn't the gentle chime of a standard campus notification. It was the harsh, urgent wail that meant immediate magical danger— the kind that got students evacuated from buildings and professors summoned from their beds in a panic.

I stumbled out of my dormitory room still half-asleep, joining the stream of confused students flowing toward the emergency assembly point in the main courtyard. The winter air was sharp against my face, helping to clear the fog of interrupted sleep.

"What's happening?" asked Sera, my roommate, who'd emerged from our room looking as bewildered as I felt.

"I don't know," I replied, scanning the crowd for any familiar faces that might have answers. "But look."

I pointed toward the Light Wing, where unusual activity was clearly visible even from our distance. Emergency magical containment barriers shimmered around the entire building, and

I could see figures in official robes moving purposefully through the corridors.

"That's not good," Sera said with considerable under-statement.

Professor Lumina appeared at my elbow as if materializing from the shadows, her usually composed expression tight with worry.

"Lyra," she said quietly, "I need you to come with me. Now."

"What's wrong?"

"Someone has broken into the Light Magical Artifacts Vault. Three major artifacts are missing, and the magical signature residue suggests this wasn't a random theft."

Ice flooded my veins. The Light Magical Artifacts Vault contained some of the most powerful and dangerous magical items in NPU's collection—objects that required specialized knowledge to even approach safely, let alone steal.

"Professor, what does this have to do with me?"

"The thief knew exactly which artifacts to take and how to bypass the security systems without triggering immediate alarms. This suggests intimate knowledge of light magic theory and vault protocols." Professor Lumina's pale eyes were grave. "Knowledge that very few students possess."

The implication hit me like a physical blow. "You think I'm a suspect."

"I think you're in danger," Professor Lumina corrected. "Lyra, whoever did this is either trying to frame you for the theft, or they're planning something that requires both the stolen artifacts and your specific expertise."

Before I could ask what she meant, Dylan appeared at my other side, looking disheveled and worried. "Lyra, are you okay? When the alarms went off, I came looking for you—"

"Mr. Vixen," Professor Lumina interrupted. "Actually, your presence is fortuitous. I believe you should hear this as well."

She gestured for us to follow her away from the crowd of students, toward a quieter area near the Crystal Gardens where we could speak without being overheard.

"The stolen artifacts," Professor Lumina began without preamble, "are the Aurora Lens, the Resonance Amplifier, and the Binding Prism."

Dylan frowned. "I don't know what any of those do."

"The Aurora Lens can project large-scale magical illusions visible from great distances," I said, my mind already working through the implications. "The Resonance Amplifier increases the power of magical bonds between compatible practitioners. And the Binding Prism..."

I trailed off as the horrifying possibility occurred to me.

"What does the Binding Prism do?" Dylan asked.

"It can forcibly create magical partnerships between unwilling participants," I whispered. "Or destroy existing magical bonds permanently."

"Dear god," Dylan breathed. "Someone's planning to weaponize partnership magic."

"That's our working theory," Professor Lumina confirmed grimly. "And there's more. The magical signature analysis suggests the thief used advanced illusion magic to avoid detection —fox shifter illusion magic, specifically."

Dylan went very pale. "Professor, you can't seriously think—"

"I don't think you're involved, Mr. Vixen. But someone clearly wants it to appear that way." Professor Lumina's expression was troubled. "The magical residue was too obvious, too cleanly fox shifter in signature. It reads like a deliberate attempt to implicate you."

"But why would someone want to frame Dylan?" I asked, though part of me already suspected the answer.

"Because Dylan's fox shifter abilities make him the perfect scapegoat," I said, understanding flooding through me. "Someone with his magical signature committing theft would reinforce every stereotype about fox shifters being untrustworthy tricksters."

We turned to find Professor Arcturus approaching, flanked by two figures I didn't recognize but whose formal robes marked them as Winter Court officials.

"Professor Arcturus," Professor Lumina said with icy politeness. "I wasn't aware the Winter Court had been invited to participate in this investigation."

"The theft of magical artifacts with partnership applications falls under Winter Court jurisdiction," Professor Arcturus replied smoothly. "Especially when the evidence points so clearly to students involved in unauthorized partnership magic experimentation."

"The evidence points to someone trying to frame those students," I said hotly. "Any competent magical investigator would recognize a planted signature when they see one."

Professor Arcturus's smile was cold and sharp. "Miss Lumina, your loyalty to your research partner is admirable but misguided. The facts are quite clear: someone with intimate knowledge of both light magic theory and fox shifter illusion techniques has stolen artifacts specifically designed for partnership magic manipulation."

"Coincidentally, just days before my Academic Review Board hearing," I added with dawning understanding. "How convenient for your case that partnership magic is dangerous."

"I hardly think I need to manufacture evidence of partnership magic's inherent instability," Professor Arcturus said with deadly calm. "Your own spectacular public failure provided ample demonstration of that."

Dylan stepped forward, his green eyes blazing with anger. "Our 'failure' was the result of pushing magical boundaries in pursuit of knowledge. Something your Winter Court friends seem determined to prevent."

"Our concern," one of the other Winter Court officials interjected, "is preventing magical catastrophes that could endanger innocent students."

"Funny," Dylan said with dangerous sweetness, "because right now it looks like your concern is manufacturing a crisis to justify shutting down research you can't control."

The tension in the air was thick enough to cut with a knife. Professor Lumina moved subtly between our group and the Winter Court officials, her posture radiating protective authority.

"Gentlemen," she said with arctic politeness, "unless you have evidence linking my students to this theft beyond circumstantial magical signatures, I suggest you focus your investigation on finding the actual perpetrator."

"We are investigating all possibilities," Professor Arcturus replied. "Including the possibility that Miss Lumina's upcoming review hearing provided motivation for desperate action."

"What's that supposed to mean?" I demanded.

"It means," Professor Arcturus said with satisfaction, "that someone facing academic disgrace and possible expulsion might be tempted to... acquire additional leverage for their situation."

The accusation hung in the air like a curse. He wasn't just suggesting that Dylan and I were involved in the theft—he was suggesting that I'd orchestrated it as some kind of desperate attempt to save my academic career.

"That's ridiculous," Dylan said flatly. "Lyra would never—"

"Wouldn't she?" Professor Arcturus's gaze fixed on me with

laser intensity. "Miss Lumina, you've repeatedly demonstrated willingness to violate university policies in pursuit of your research goals. Is it so difficult to believe you might escalate to theft when academic pressure mounted?"

"Yes," I said with quiet fury, "it is. Because unlike some people, I actually believe in the principles of ethical magical research."

"Ethical research," Professor Arcturus repeated mockingly. "Is that what you call magical experimentation that resulted in campus-wide magical disruption and the destruction of a partnership bond?"

"I call it learning from mistakes and working to prevent them in the future," I shot back. "Which is more than I can say for people who would rather suppress knowledge than risk admitting they might be wrong."

Professor Lumina placed a warning hand on my arm. "Lyra."

"No," I said, shaking off her restraint. "I'm tired of being polite to people who are more interested in control than truth."

I stepped closer to Professor Arcturus, meeting his cold gaze with defiant determination.

"You want to know what I think happened here? I think someone with access to Winter Court resources and detailed knowledge of NPU's security systems orchestrated this theft specifically to frame Dylan and me. I think this is a manufactured crisis designed to justify shutting down partnership magic research permanently."

"That's a serious accusation, Miss Lumina."

"It's a serious situation, Professor Arcturus. Someone has stolen powerful magical artifacts that could be used to cause real harm to students. But instead of focusing on finding the actual thief, you're here trying to pin the blame on the most convenient scapegoats."

"The most obvious suspects," Professor Arcturus corrected coldly.

"The most inconvenient researchers," I countered. "Dylan and I have proven that partnership magic can be both powerful and stable. We've developed theoretical frameworks that could revolutionize magical education. And that threatens everything you've built your authority on."

The Winter Court officials exchanged glances that suggested I'd hit closer to the truth than they were comfortable with.

"Miss Lumina," Professor Arcturus said with dangerous quiet, "you are making accusations that border on sedition."

"I'm making observations that border on truth."

"Enough." Professor Lumina's voice cut through the tension like a blade. "This conversation has become unproductive. Gentlemen, unless you have specific evidence warranting the detention of my students, I suggest you return to your investigation."

"The investigation will continue," Professor Arcturus said, his gaze never leaving my face. "And Miss Lumina, I hope for your sake that the evidence doesn't support the conclusions it currently suggests."

"Is that a threat?"

"It's a warning. The Winter Court takes theft of magical artifacts very seriously. Especially when those artifacts could be used to destabilize the established magical order."

After the Winter Court officials left, the three of us stood in silence for a long moment, processing what had just occurred.

"Well," Dylan said finally, "that was terrifying."

"It was revealing," I said grimly. "Did you notice that Professor Arcturus knew exactly which artifacts had been stolen? He mentioned their partnership magic applications before Professor Lumina had specified what they were used for."

Professor Lumina nodded slowly. "I noticed. Along with the

fact that he seemed more concerned with building a case against you two than with recovering the stolen items."

"So what do we do?" Dylan asked.

"We find the real thief," I said with determination. "Before they can use those artifacts for whatever they're actually planning."

"Lyra," Professor Lumina said carefully, "I understand your desire to clear your names, but this is extremely dangerous. Whoever orchestrated this theft has significant magical resources and Winter Court connections. They're not going to hesitate to eliminate anyone who threatens their plans."

"Then we'd better make sure we find them before they find us," Dylan said grimly.

I looked at him—this brave, brilliant man who'd already risked so much to stand beside me—and felt a fierce surge of protective determination.

"Dylan, you don't have to—"

"Yes, I do," he interrupted. "Lyra, we're partners. That means we face whatever comes next together."

"Even if it means going up against the Winter Court directly?"

"Especially then." His smile was equal parts affection and stubborn resolve. "Besides, I'm curious to see what partnership magic without magical bonds can accomplish when it's properly motivated."

Despite everything—the theft, the accusations, the very real danger we were now facing—I found myself smiling back.

"In that case," I said, "I suppose we'd better get started. Because whoever's behind this has made one crucial mistake."

"What's that?"

"They've given us a common enemy." I looked toward the Light Wing, where the emergency barriers were still shimmering ominously. "And nothing motivates partnership quite like someone trying to destroy what you've built together."

As we began planning our investigation into the theft, I couldn't shake the feeling that this was exactly what Professor Arcturus had been waiting for—an excuse to escalate from academic pressure to criminal accusations.

But what he might not have anticipated was that Dylan and I were no longer the uncertain students who'd stumbled into partnership magic by accident.

We were partners by choice, researchers by training, and now, apparently, detectives by necessity.

And we were going to prove that some partnerships were too strong to be broken by theft, accusations, or even the Winter Court itself.

The question was: would we figure out who was really behind this before they finished whatever plan required stealing partnership magic artifacts?

And more importantly: what were they planning to do with the power to forcibly create—or destroy—magical bonds?

The answers to those questions, I suspected, were going to determine not just our academic futures, but the future of partnership magic research itself.

Time to find out exactly how far we were willing to go to protect what we'd discovered together.

CHAPTER EIGHTEEN
TRUST TESTED

DYLAN

The investigation was going nowhere, and I could see the strain wearing on Lyra with each passing hour.

We'd spent the past two days following leads that evaporated under scrutiny, analyzing magical signatures that told us nothing we didn't already know, and trying to piece together a timeline that made sense of the theft. The Aurora Lens, Resonance Amplifier, and Binding Prism had vanished from a vault that should have been impossible to breach without leaving massive magical traces.

Yet somehow, the only evidence the official investigation had found pointed directly at me.

"This doesn't make sense," Lyra muttered, hunched over a stack of magical forensics reports in her Observatory. Dark circles shadowed her eyes, and her usually perfect posture had given way to the exhausted slump of someone who'd been pushing too hard for too long. "The magical signature is too clean, too obviously fox shifter. Real thieves don't leave calling cards."

"Unless they want to be caught," I pointed out, though even as I said it, the explanation felt hollow.

"But you wouldn't want to be caught. And you're too smart to leave such obvious evidence even if you were somehow involved, which you're not." Lyra rubbed her temples with shaking fingers. "The whole thing feels orchestrated."

I watched her struggle with the puzzle, noting the way her brilliant mind kept circling back to the same impossible conclusion: that someone was deliberately framing me. What I couldn't figure out was why that possibility seemed to be causing her so much distress—beyond the obvious implications for our investigation.

She kept glancing at me when she thought I wasn't looking, her expression cycling through emotions I couldn't identify. There was something she wasn't telling me, something that was eating at her from the inside.

"Lyra," I said carefully, "you know I didn't steal those artifacts, right?"

She looked up from the reports, her pale blue eyes wide with what looked almost like relief at the direct question. "Of course I know that. Dylan, you spent your entire winter break recreating my research and learning advanced light magic. You're not exactly the type to turn to theft when things get difficult."

But even as she said it, I caught the slight hesitation, the way her gaze didn't quite meet mine directly.

"Then why do you look like you haven't slept in days?"

"Because someone wants to burn down everything we've built —and they're using you to light the match," she said with brittle intensity. "Because whoever's behind this theft is using it as a weapon against partnership magic research. Because the Winter Court is breathing down our necks and my Review Board hearing is tomorrow and if we can't prove your innocence, they're going to use this as justification to shut down all partnership magic studies permanently."

"And?"

"And what?"

"There's something else," I said, moving closer to where she sat surrounded by scattered papers and empty coffee cups. "Lyra, I know you well enough to recognize when you're holding something back. What aren't you telling me?"

For a moment, she just stared at me, her expression cycling through emotions I couldn't identify. Then, with the careful deliberation of someone approaching something dangerous, she reached beneath the stack of reports.

"I wasn't going to show you this," she said quietly, her voice thick with something that might have been guilt. "I kept telling myself it didn't matter, that I knew you better than some magical forensics analysis could suggest. That questioning you would be betraying everything we've built together."

Ice filled my stomach. "What is it?"

"The detailed breakdown of the magical signature found at the theft site." Lyra's hands trembled as she pulled out a single sheet of parchment. "Dylan, I've been staring at this for hours, trying to find some explanation that doesn't make me question everything I thought I knew about you."

"The detailed breakdown of the magical signature found at the theft site." Lyra's voice was steady, but her hands trembled slightly as she handed me the parchment. "Dylan, the magic they found... it's not just fox shifter illusion work. It's specifically your magical signature."

The words hit like a physical blow, but the real pain came from seeing the doubt in Lyra's eyes—doubt about me, about us, about everything we'd built together.

For a moment, I couldn't speak. Couldn't process that the

person who knew me better than anyone was asking if I might be lying to her face.

"That's impossible," I said finally, but my voice sounded weak even to my own ears.

"I know." The words came out strained, like they'd been forced through something tight and painful. "Dylan, I know it's impossible. But the evidence..."

"Lyra, I was in my dormitory room when the theft occurred. Kieran can vouch for me—we were working on that transfiguration essay for Professor Moonheart until nearly two in the morning."

"I know," she repeated, but I caught the way she couldn't quite look at me directly.

"Do you?"

The question hung between us, loaded with implications I wasn't sure I was ready to confront.

"Dylan," Lyra said carefully, "how well do you understand your own magical abilities? I mean, really understand them?"

"What kind of question is that?"

"The kind that matters when we're trying to figure out how your exact magical signature ended up at a crime scene you weren't present for." Lyra's academic composure was slipping, revealing the fear underneath. "Dylan, is it possible that someone could have... I don't know, duplicated your magic somehow? Created an artificial version of your signature?"

"I don't think so. Fox shifter magic is pretty distinctive, and the chaos patterns are supposed to be impossible to replicate artificially."

"What about during our partnership bond? Could someone have recorded your magical signature then and found a way to reproduce it later?"

The suggestion made my skin crawl, but more than that, it

triggered a half-forgotten memory. "You know, there was something..." I paused, trying to grasp the elusive recollection. "During one of our Observatory sessions, I remember noticing a strange shimmer in the air. Like someone had cast a very subtle observation charm."

Lyra straightened. "When?"

"A few weeks before our bond shattered. I mentioned it to you, but you said it was probably just aurora light reflecting off the crystal surfaces." The memory was getting clearer now, bringing with it an uncomfortable realization. "But thinking back, the shimmer moved. Like it was following our magical connection."

"Someone was watching us," Lyra said with growing certainty. "Recording our magical signatures, studying our bond patterns."

"I think someone with Winter Court resources and detailed knowledge of partnership magic theory might have found ways to observe us that we never detected." Lyra's voice was getting sharper, more strained. "Your admission was sponsored by someone in the Winter Court. Your magic started fluctuating when partnership research gained attention. Now your signature shows up at a theft site. Dylan, the pattern... it's there."

I stared at her, processing not just the implications of what she was suggesting, but the fact that she'd been putting this pattern together without telling me.

"And you think I might be part of that pattern," I said quietly.

"I think you might not know everything about your own situation." The words seemed to break something open inside her. "Because right now, I don't even know if I know myself."

"That's..." I struggled to find words adequate to the betrayal she was suggesting. "That's monstrous."

"It would be effective," Lyra said grimly. "Destroy our partnership bond, steal our magical signatures, then use them to commit crimes that would justify shutting down all partnership magic research. It's exactly the kind of long-term strategy the Winter Court would employ."

"But you can't prove it."

"No. And that's the problem." Lyra stood up abruptly, pacing to the Observatory's eastern window. "Dylan, the evidence against you is compelling. Not just the magical signature, but the timing, the specialized knowledge required, the fact that you've been publicly associated with unauthorized partnership magic experimentation."

"Lyra, where is this going?"

She turned to face me, and for the first time since I'd known her, I saw real doubt in her eyes. Not academic uncertainty, but personal doubt about me, about us, about everything she'd thought she could trust.

"I need you to tell me the truth," she said quietly. "About everything. About your magical abilities, about your family connections, about whether there's any possibility—any possibility at all—that you could be involved in this theft."

The words felt like a knife between my ribs. After everything we'd been through, everything we'd built together, she was asking if I might be lying to her.

I stepped back, the physical distance suddenly feeling necessary. "You think I'm lying to you."

"You're asking me to throw out logic, training—everything I've built my career on—for a feeling."

I sat in stunned silence, trying to process what she was really asking. Not just whether I was guilty of theft, but whether our entire relationship had been built on deception.

"Lyra," I said finally, "do you remember what you told me about partnership magic? About how true magical compatibility can't be faked or forced?"

"Yes."

"Do you remember how our magic felt when it connected? The way it recognized something in each other that we didn't even know we were looking for?"

"Dylan—"

"Do you remember the way your magic responded when we kissed two days ago? How it created aurora patterns that were more beautiful than anything we'd achieved during our formal partnership bond?"

"That's not the point—"

"It's exactly the point." I stood up, moving to face her across the space that suddenly felt like a chasm. "Lyra, magic doesn't lie. Individual magical signatures can be duplicated, partnership bonds can be manipulated, even memories can be altered. But the way two people's magic responds to genuine emotional connection? That can't be faked."

"You're asking me to trust magic over evidence."

"I'm asking you to trust what you know to be true over what someone wants you to believe." I reached for her hands, noting the way she hesitated before allowing the contact. "Lyra, if I were a Winter Court agent, if everything between us had been orchestrated manipulation, do you really think my magic would have responded to yours the way it did?"

"I don't know," she whispered, and the admission seemed to break something inside her. "Dylan, I want to trust you. I want to believe that what we have together is real. But the evidence..."

"The evidence is circumstantial at best and deliberately misleading at worst." I squeezed her hands gently, trying to anchor her to something more substantial than forensic reports and suspicion. "Lyra, look at me."

She met my eyes reluctantly.

"I didn't steal those artifacts. I've never worked for the Winter

Court. Everything I've told you about my feelings, my intentions, my commitment to our partnership—all of it is true." I paused, making sure she was really hearing me. "But more than that, you know it's true. Not because of evidence or logic or magical forensics, but because you know me. You know who I am when no one else is watching."

"Do I?"

"You know I'm the kind of person who spent his entire winter break recreating your research because I couldn't stand the thought of you losing something important. You know I'm the kind of person who learned advanced light magic just to prove that our connection wasn't dependent on magical convenience. You know I'm the kind of person who would rather face criminal charges than let you fight this alone."

Lyra was quiet for a long moment, studying my face as if she could read the truth written there.

"The magical signature match is exact, Dylan. Not similar, not reminiscent of your magic—exact. Down to the chaos pattern fluctuations that should be impossible to replicate."

"Then someone found a way to replicate the impossible," I said firmly. "Or someone recorded my magical signature during our partnership bond and found a way to reproduce it artificially. Or someone with Winter Court resources developed technology we don't know about. What I didn't do is steal powerful magical artifacts to use against the research we've both sacrificed so much to protect."

"You're asking me to ignore physical evidence in favor of emotional conviction."

"I'm asking you to remember that the most important discoveries can't be measured by conventional means." I moved closer, until we were standing near enough that our magical auras began to overlap. "Lyra, what does your magic tell you about mine?

Right now, with no external influences or artificial enhancements —what does your instinct say?"

She closed her eyes, and I felt her magical awareness extend toward mine. Not the formal diagnostic techniques she used for academic research, but the intuitive recognition that had made our partnership possible in the first place.

The moment our magical signatures touched, aurora patterns began painting themselves across the Observatory walls. Not the dramatic displays we'd created during passionate moments, but something subtler, more fundamental. The quiet harmony of two magical systems that recognized each other on a level deeper than conscious thought.

"It feels like coming home," Lyra said softly, her eyes still closed. "Like magic the way it's supposed to be."

"Could that feeling be artificially created?"

"No," she admitted. "Individual magical signatures can be duplicated, but the resonance between compatible magics... that comes from emotional and spiritual alignment that can't be faked."

"Then trust that," I said quietly. "Trust what you know to be true, not what someone wants you to doubt."

When Lyra opened her eyes, some of the tension had gone out of her posture. "Dylan, if you're not involved in the theft, then someone with incredibly sophisticated magical resources is going to extraordinary lengths to frame you."

"Yes."

"Which means we're not just dealing with opportunistic criminals. We're dealing with people who have access to Winter Court magic and detailed knowledge of our partnership research."

"Also yes."

"And they're willing to violate the most fundamental principles of magical ethics to achieve their goals."

"Which tells us exactly how dangerous they consider partnership magic to be," I pointed out. "Lyra, people don't go to these lengths to suppress something harmless. They're afraid of what we represent."

"What do we represent?"

"Proof that magical education's foundational assumptions are wrong. Evidence that students don't need institutional permission to achieve extraordinary things. A demonstration that magical partnerships can be both powerful and voluntary."

Lyra nodded slowly. "Everything that threatens their authority."

"Everything that threatens their control," I corrected. "Which means we're not just fighting to clear my name or save your academic career. We're fighting for the future of magical education itself."

"No pressure, then."

"None at all." I smiled, relieved beyond measure to see the return of her dry humor. "So, are we partners in this investigation? Or do I need to prove my innocence before you'll trust me to watch your back?"

"We're partners," Lyra said without hesitation. "Dylan, I'm sorry I doubted you. The evidence was so convincing, and I've been so afraid of losing everything we've built together..."

"You don't need to apologize for asking hard questions. That's what makes you a good researcher." I pulled her into my arms, noting how perfectly she fit against me. "But next time you're worried about something, talk to me about it before you torture yourself with worst-case scenarios."

"Deal. Though I should probably warn you, I have several more worst-case scenarios I've been working through."

"Such as?"

"Such as the possibility that whoever stole those artifacts

plans to use them at my Review Board hearing tomorrow. Think about it—the Aurora Lens for large-scale illusions, the Resonance Amplifier for enhancing magical effects, and the Binding Prism for demonstrating the 'dangers' of partnership magic."

I felt the blood drain from my face. "They're going to stage a magical disaster during your hearing."

"It would be the perfect capstone to their campaign against partnership magic research. Manufacture a crisis that appears to prove their point about inherent instability, then use it to justify permanent restrictions on the field."

"Lyra, if they're planning something that dramatic, they're not going to care about collateral damage. People could get seriously hurt."

"I know." Her expression was grim but determined. "Which is why we need to figure out how to stop them before tomorrow afternoon."

"Any ideas?"

"Actually, yes." Lyra moved to her central platform, calling up holographic displays of the stolen artifacts and their theoretical applications. "But you're not going to like it."

"Try me."

"We're going to have to beat them at their own game. Use our knowledge of partnership magic theory to turn whatever trap they're planning against them."

"How?"

"By giving them exactly what they think they want—a public demonstration of partnership magic's power—and making sure it proves the opposite of what they expect."

I studied the artifacts rotating in the holographic display, my mind already working through the implications of what she was suggesting.

"Lyra, that's incredibly dangerous. If we miscalculate, if they have contingencies we haven't anticipated..."

"Then we'll face the consequences together," she said simply. "Dylan, we've spent months proving that partnership magic can create beauty instead of chaos. Tomorrow, we're going to prove it can create hope instead of fear."

"And if we're wrong?"

"Then at least we'll go down fighting for something we believe in." Lyra's smile was fierce and unafraid. "Besides, I have complete faith in my partner's ability to find creative solutions to impossible problems."

"Your partner being the guy who was just accused of magical theft?"

"My partner being the guy who chose to rebuild rather than retreat when everything seemed lost." She reached for my hands, and immediately the Observatory filled with gentle aurora light. "The guy who proved that real partnership is stronger than magical bonds, more powerful than institutional opposition, and more valuable than safety."

"No pressure at all," I said again, but this time I was smiling.

"None whatsoever." Lyra's expression grew serious. "Dylan, are you really willing to risk everything on a plan that could back-fire spectacularly?"

"I'm willing to risk everything to protect what we've built together," I said without hesitation. "Besides, what's the worst that could happen?"

"We could be expelled, arrested, magically drained, or killed."

"Okay, so there's some downside potential."

"Considerable downside potential."

"But also considerable upside potential," I pointed out. "If we pull this off, we don't just clear my name and save your research privileges. We expose whoever's really behind this conspiracy and prove that partnership magic deserves a place in magical education."

"And if we don't pull it off?"

"Then we'll have given it our best shot." I squeezed her hands gently. "Lyra, I'd rather fail attempting something extraordinary than succeed at something ordinary."

"That," she said with a grin that was part admiration, part exasperation, "is the most fox shifter thing you've ever said."

"I'll take that as a compliment."

"You should." Lyra turned back to the holographic displays, her expression shifting into the focused intensity I recognized as her planning mode. "Alright, if we're going to do this, we need to figure out exactly how to turn a staged magical disaster into a demonstration of partnership magic's stability and beauty."

"Any initial thoughts?"

"Several. But first, I need to ask you something important."

"What?"

"Dylan, are you prepared to trust me completely tomorrow? To follow my lead even if my plan seems impossible or dangerous?"

"Always."

"Even if it means using partnership magic techniques we've never tested? Even if it means putting ourselves at the center of whatever magical chaos they're planning to create?"

"Especially then." I moved to stand beside her at the platform, our combined presence making the theoretical displays more dynamic and alive. "Lyra, we've faced magical disasters before. We've survived partnership bond destruction, institutional opposition, and criminal accusations. Whatever they throw at us tomorrow, we'll handle it together."

"Together," she agreed. "Though I should probably warn you, my plan involves several illegal applications of magical theory, at least three violations of university policy, and one technique that technically doesn't exist yet."

"Sounds perfect for us."

"I thought you might say that." Lyra's smile was bright with determination and affection. "Alright, partner. Let's save partnership magic."

As we began planning what was probably going to be the most spectacular magical demonstration in NPU history, I couldn't help but think that whoever had tried to frame me had made one crucial miscalculation.

They'd assumed that criminal accusations would drive Lyra and me apart, that doubt and suspicion would destroy what we'd built together.

Instead, they'd given us something even more powerful than magical partnership: absolute certainty that we were fighting for something worth defending.

Tomorrow, we'd find out whether that certainty was enough to change the course of magical education forever.

Or whether we'd both go down in spectacular, beautiful, partnership magic flames.

Together, we were unpredictable, uncontainable, and unstoppable. And that, I realized, was the kind of magic they'd never understand—because it didn't come from rules. It came from *us*.

CHAPTER NINETEEN
POWER UNLEASHED

DYLAN

The Review Board hearing was at two o'clock. That gave us four hours to catch a thief, recover three stolen artifacts, and prepare the most important presentation in partnership magic history.

No pressure at all.

"Are you sure about this plan?" I asked Lyra for the third time as we made our way through the pre-dawn corridors toward the Light Wing. Our footsteps echoed, joined by the low hum of magical heating systems keeping the castle warm.

"No," Lyra said. "But it's the best we've got."

Our plan? Break into the Light Wing, find the artifacts, and not get caught. It was risky, borderline illegal, and the kind of thing only two desperate students would attempt.

"Besides," Lyra continued, "your illusion magic has developed considerably since we started working together. The individual light constructs you've mastered should be more than sufficient for creating visual camouflage."

"Assuming I can maintain them under pressure."

"You can." Her voice carried complete confidence. "Dylan, you've spent months learning to cast complex magic without partnership enhancement. Trust yourself."

We reached the Light Wing's service entrance, where Lyra activated a small scanning device she'd borrowed from her Observatory equipment. The magical resonance detector would help us identify any unusual energy signatures that might indicate hidden artifacts.

"Alright," she said quietly, studying the readout. "I'm detecting faint traces of aurora magic coming from the upper storage levels. That could be residue from the Aurora Lens."

"Or it could be standard Light Wing ambient energy."

"Only one way to find out."

I closed my eyes and reached for my magic, crafting an illusion that would bend light around us and make us effectively invisible to casual observation. The spell required significant concentration, but it felt stable, controlled—proof that months of systematic practice had paid off.

"Nice work," Lyra murmured as we faded from view. "I can barely see you, and I'm standing right next to you."

"Thanks. Let's hope it holds up when we encounter whatever security measures they have in place."

We made our way up the service stairs, moving carefully to avoid making noise that might attract attention. The Light Wing felt different in the pre-dawn darkness—more mysterious, more dangerous, like a place where secrets lived in the shadows between magical experiments.

"There," Lyra whispered, pointing to a door marked 'Advanced Research Storage - Authorized Personnel Only.' "That's where they'd keep anything too sensitive for the regular vaults."

I maintained the illusion while Lyra worked on the door's

locking mechanisms. Her theoretical knowledge of magical security systems proved surprisingly practical when applied to actual breaking and entering.

"Got it," she said as the door swung open silently. "Though I should probably mention that bypassing NPU security wards is definitely grounds for expulsion."

"Add it to the list of academic violations we're committing today."

The storage room beyond was obsessively organized—except for one corner, where someone had clearly been working. Gaps in shelves, magical residue, signs of recent use.

"Dylan, look at this." Lyra pointed to the disrupted section. "Someone's been using this space as a workshop."

I let the illusion drop, needing to focus my magical energy on the scanning spell Lyra had taught me. Immediately, I could sense the lingering traces of powerful magical artifacts—aurora light projection, resonance amplification, and something that felt like forced magical bonding.

"They were here," I said. "All three. But someone moved them."

"Recently moved," Lyra added, studying her detection equipment. "The magical signatures are still warm. Dylan, whoever took them moved them within the last few hours."

"Which means they're probably somewhere in the castle, getting ready for whatever they're planning to do during your hearing."

"The question is where." Lyra frowned at her scanner. "The Aurora Lens would need line of sight to the hearing room for maximum effect. The Resonance Amplifier would need to be close enough to enhance any magical demonstrations. And the Binding Prism..."

"Would need to be positioned where it could affect everyone

present," I finished. "Lyra, they're not just planning to stage a magical disaster. They're planning to use forced magical bonding to make it look like partnership magic is inherently dangerous to unwilling participants."

The implications were horrifying. Forced magical bonding was one of the most serious crimes in magical law—a violation of personal autonomy that could cause permanent psychological and magical damage.

"We need to find those artifacts before the hearing begins," Lyra said with urgent determination.

"Any ideas about where they might be?"

"Actually, yes." She consulted her scanner again, then looked up with grim satisfaction. "The magical resonance patterns suggest they're somewhere with direct access to the hearing chamber but hidden from normal observation. Somewhere like..."

"The gallery above the Crystal Amphitheater," I said, under-standing immediately. "Perfect line of sight, acoustically connected, and normally empty during formal proceedings."

"Exactly. Dylan, if I'm right, we have about two hours to get up there, neutralize whatever trap they've set, and figure out how to turn their plan against them."

"And if you're wrong?"

"Then we'll have spent our last few hours of freedom on a wild goose chase instead of preparing better defenses."

I considered this for a moment. "You know what? I like those odds."

We made our way back through the Light Wing and across campus toward the Crystal Amphitheater, moving carefully to avoid the increasing number of early-rising students and faculty. The morning was crisp and clear, with aurora patterns painting the sky in shades of green and gold that reminded me of the magic Lyra and I created together.

"Dylan," Lyra said as we approached the amphitheater's service entrance, "I need to tell you something important before we go in there."

"What?"

"If this goes wrong—if we're caught, if the plan backfires, if whoever's behind this has contingencies we haven't anticipated —I want you to know that trusting you yesterday was the easiest decision I've ever made."

The simple statement hit me harder than any declaration of love could have.

"Even after seeing the forensics evidence? Even knowing that trusting me meant ignoring logical analysis in favor of emotional conviction?"

"Especially then." Lyra smiled, and the warmth in her expression made my chest ache with affection. "Dylan, logic and analysis can tell you about magical signatures and circumstantial evidence. But they can't tell you about character, or integrity, or the way someone's magic feels when it recognizes something true."

"And my magic feels true to you?"

"Your magic feels like home to me," she said simply. "Like everything I've been looking for without knowing I was searching."

Before I could respond, she was moving toward the amphitheater entrance, leaving me to follow with the words echoing in my mind like a benediction.

Like home.

The gallery above the Crystal Amphitheater was exactly where we'd expected to find evidence of the theft, but what we discovered there was worse than anything we'd imagined.

The stolen artifacts had been arranged in a precise triangle around a central platform that overlooked the hearing chamber below. But more than that, they'd been modified—enhanced with additional magical components that turned them from powerful but controllable tools into something approaching weapons.

"Mother of magic," Lyra breathed, her scanner practically vibrating with alarm as she took readings. "Dylan, they've jury-rigged these artifacts into a feedback amplification system. When activated, they won't just create illusions or enhance magical bonds—they'll force magical connections between every person in the amphitheater."

"Forced connections that will probably be unstable and painful," I said, studying the setup with growing horror.

"More than painful. Potentially lethal." Lyra's face was pale with understanding. "Dylan, if this system activates during a room full of professors and administrators, the magical backlash could kill dozens of people."

"And whoever survives will have experienced firsthand the 'dangers' of partnership magic gone wrong."

"It's the perfect false flag operation. Create a magical disaster, blame it on partnership magic research, and use the tragedy to justify permanent restrictions on the field."

I moved closer to examine the central platform, noting the way the artifacts had been positioned to focus their combined energy downward toward the hearing chamber.

"Lyra, this setup is sophisticated. Whoever designed this knows advanced magical engineering and has access to rare components. This isn't just someone with Winter Court connections—this is someone with serious resources and technical expertise."

"Which narrows our suspect list considerably." Lyra was taking detailed scans of the modified artifacts. "Dylan, I think I know how to disable this system, but it's going to require precise

magical work while under pressure. Are you up for some collaborative spellcasting?"

"With you? Always."

"Good, because we're about to have company."

I heard it too—footsteps on the gallery stairs, approaching
with the measured pace of someone who belonged here. Someone
who was coming to make final preparations for whatever was
scheduled to happen during the hearing.

"Hide," Lyra whispered, pointing to a section of gallery
seating that would provide concealment.

I activated my illusion magic, bending light around both of us
just as the gallery door opened to admit a figure I recognized with
shocked disbelief.

Professor Ember from Elemental Studies stepped into the
gallery, moving with obvious familiarity toward the artifact array.
She was followed by someone I didn't recognize—a tall, pale
figure in Winter Court robes whose magical signature felt like
arctic wind and old authority.

"The calibrations are complete?" the Winter Court official
asked.

"Everything's ready," Professor Ember replied, making small
adjustments to the Resonance Amplifier. Her voice was tight with
something deeper—bitterness, maybe even fear. "When Miss
Lumina presents, the Lens projects false success. Then the Prism
activates—forced bonds, chaos, and a room full of victims
blaming partnership magic."

"And the forced connections will destabilize immediately?"

"Within minutes. The backlash will be attributed to partnership magic's instability, and survivors will testify to the dangers of
unsupervised bonding research. You think this is about power?
It's survival. The Winter Court doesn't tolerate dissent."

She talked about deaths like logistics. This wasn't politics—it was premeditated murder.

"Professor Arcturus will be pleased," the Winter Court official said with satisfaction. "The partnership magic threat will be eliminated permanently, and the Winter Court's authority over magical education will be unquestioned."

"What about the students who discovered the original research?" Professor Ember asked. "Miss Lumina and Mr. Vixen?"

"Unfortunate casualties of their own dangerous experiments," the official replied coldly. "Their deaths will serve as a warning to future students who might be tempted to pursue unauthorized magical research."

I felt Lyra's sharp intake of breath beside me, and had to resist the urge to comfort her. Hearing our deaths discussed so casually was horrifying, but it also provided crucial information about the scope of the conspiracy against us.

"The hearing begins in ninety minutes," Professor Ember said, checking a magical timepiece. "I'll remain here to monitor the system activation. You should return to Professor Arcturus and confirm that everything is proceeding according to plan."

"Very well. Remember—the appearance of spontaneous magical disaster is crucial. No one must suspect deliberate intervention."

After the Winter Court official left, Professor Ember settled into a monitoring position where she could observe both the artifact array and the hearing chamber below. She activated several additional magical devices that looked like recording equipment —apparently, they wanted detailed documentation of whatever disaster they were planning to create.

I caught Lyra's eye and saw my own determination reflected there. We had ninety minutes to disable a magical weapon system, gather evidence of the conspiracy, and somehow turn the situation to our advantage.

Time to find out what partnership magic could accomplish when it was properly motivated.

I began crafting illusions while Lyra analyzed the artifact modifications. Working without formal magical partnership, we moved like dancers following music only we could hear.

"There," Lyra whispered, pointing to magical conduits connecting the artifacts. "If we disrupt the energy flow between the Aurora Lens and the Binding Prism, the entire system should become unstable."

"Unstable how?"

"The kind that makes artifacts malfunction spectacularly without life-threatening backlash."

"I like that kind of unstable."

I moved closer to the conduit network, maintaining my illusions while preparing to cast the most precise magical working of my life. The spell required threading chaotic energy through a gap barely wider than a hair, disrupting the connection without triggering defensive systems.

"Dylan," Lyra said urgently, "Professor Ember is moving. I think she suspects something."

I looked up to see the Elemental Studies professor scanning the gallery with obvious suspicion, her hand moving toward what looked like an alarm crystal.

"She can sense our magic," I realized. "The illusions are holding, but she's detecting the energy fluctuations from our spellwork."

"Can you maintain visual concealment while I create a magical dampening field?"

"For how long?"

"Long enough to finish disabling the system and gather evidence of the conspiracy."

"Do it."

Lyra began weaving a complex suppression spell that would mask our magical signatures while allowing us to continue casting. The theoretical elegance of her approach was breathtaking—she was essentially creating a zone of magical silence around us without interfering with our own spellwork.

Meanwhile, I focused everything I had on the conduit disruption spell. Threading chaotic energy through precise pathways, using the systematic approach Lyra had taught me to guide natural magical instincts toward specific targets.

The moment my magic touched the connection between artifacts, the conduit network sparked and failed. My illusions flickered as I divided attention between concealment and sabotage. And in the magical feedback from the failing system, I sensed something that made my blood freeze.

I froze. Resonance patterns weren't just here—they echoed from across campus like war drums. "Lyra... there are more. At least three. They're not targeting your hearing—they're targeting the whole university."

The scope of the conspiracy was staggering. Not just framing us for theft, not just disrupting partnership magic research, but creating a magical catastrophe that would justify Winter Court control over all magical education.

"Dylan, we have to warn everyone. If those other arrays activate—"

"I know." I looked at the failing system around us, at Professor Ember who was now actively searching for intruders, at the evidence of conspiracy we'd gathered. "But first, we need to make sure this particular array can't be repaired."

"What are you thinking?"

"I'm thinking it's time to find out what happens when fox shifter chaos magic meets a carefully balanced magical engineering project."

"Dylan, if you overload that system, the feedback could—"

"Could create a very visible demonstration of what happens when someone tries to weaponize partnership magic artifacts," I finished. "Lyra, trust me."

She met my eyes, and I saw understanding pass between us. Not just about the magical working I was proposing, but about the choice we were making to stand up against forces that would rather commit mass murder than admit they might be wrong.

"Together?" she asked.

"Always together."

I reached for the deepest levels of my chaos magic while Lyra provided structural framework to direct that energy toward maximum drama with minimum danger. Together, we poured everything into the failing artifact array.

The result was spectacular.

I hadn't meant for the sky to tell the truth. But our magic had —spelling "Winter Court Conspiracy" in glowing letters above NPU while the Aurora Lens projected wild, beautiful patterns that told partnership magic's real story. The Resonance Amplifier broadcast our combined signature to every sensitive mage within miles. And the Binding Prism shattered completely.

Chaos magic was honest like that.

The magical explosion was visible from anywhere on campus, accompanied by crystal chimes and aurora wind.

"Well," Lyra said as alarms rang throughout NPU, "I think Professor Ember's plan has been disrupted."

Professor Ember stared at us in shock and fury. "You," she snarled. "You've ruined everything."

"Actually," I said, "we just saved everyone."

The gallery doors burst open. Professor Lumina entered with faculty and NPU security, taking in the destroyed artifacts and Professor Ember with magic crackling around her hands.

"Professor Ember," Professor Lumina said with arctic calm, "you're under arrest."

As campus security restrained Professor Ember, Lyra slipped her hand into mine.

"Nice work, partner."

"You too. Though I have to ask—how did Professor Lumina know to bring backup?"

"Because," Professor Lumina said, approaching with mixed pride and exasperation, "magical explosions visible from three provinces tend to attract attention. When aurora patterns start spelling accusations in fifty-foot letters, it's hard to ignore."

While we'd been preparing our sabotage, Lyra had sent a silent alert through the Observatory's grid to Professor Lumina. If this went wrong, she'd wanted someone to have evidence.

"I believe you have a hearing in one hour," Professor Lumina continued. "Though I suspect the circumstances have changed considerably."

"How so?" I asked.

"Well, Professor Arcturus will find it difficult to argue that partnership magic is inherently dangerous when you've just used it to prevent a mass casualty event." Her smile was satisfied but cautious. "However, this is far from over. Professor Ember was working under Winter Court authority, which means they have legal backing for their actions."

"Legal backing for attempted murder?" Lyra asked incredulously.

"Legal backing for 'magical safety enforcement,'" Professor Lumina corrected grimly. "They'll claim Professor Ember was conducting a necessary test of partnership magic's stability, and that your interference prevented proper safety protocols."

The realization hit like cold water. "They're going to spin this as us being the dangerous ones."

"Almost certainly. Which means your hearing isn't just about academic reinstatement anymore—it's about proving that partnership magic can be both powerful and responsible."

I looked at Lyra, seeing my own determination reflected in her pale eyes. We'd caught one conspirator and prevented one disaster, but the real fight was just beginning.

"Then we'd better make sure our presentation is spectacular," Lyra said.

"Indeed. Though I should warn you—Professor Arcturus will undoubtedly have contingency plans. He's not the type to accept defeat gracefully."

As we gathered evidence from the destroyed artifact array and prepared to face whatever came next, I realized that catching Professor Ember had been the easy part.

Now we had to convince the entire NPU administration that partnership magic deserved a future.

And we had less than an hour to prepare for the most important presentation of our lives.

CHAPTER TWENTY
THE CLAIM

LYRA

The Crystal Amphitheater glittered with festive light, transformed by the Spring Equinox Festival into a celebration of academic achievement. But to me, it felt like a battlefield. Every floating crystal flower, every aurora ribbon dancing through the air like living things, was a distraction from the fact that my future—and partnership magic itself—hung in the balance. What should have been a private Review Board hearing had somehow evolved into a public spectacle, which meant that half of NPU seemed to have crammed into the gallery seats to witness my potential academic downfall.

"Nervous?" Dylan asked quietly, his hand finding mine as we sat in the front row of the amphitheater's lower tier.

"Terrified," I admitted, watching as professors, administrators, and Winter Court officials took their places on the raised platform. "This was supposed to be a simple hearing about reinstating my research privileges. Now it feels like..."

"Like a trial?" Dylan's green eyes were warm with understanding. "Lyra, after what we discovered about Professor Ember and the artifact conspiracy, this isn't just about your academic standing anymore. It's about proving that partnership magic deserves a future."

The morning's revelations had spread through campus like frostfire. Professor Ember's arrest, the discovery of the modified artifacts, the evidence of Winter Court manipulation—all of it had transformed what should have been a routine academic review into something approaching a public referendum on partnership magic research.

"Miss Lumina," Professor Blitzen's voice cut through the ambient chatter as the formal proceedings began. "Please approach the podium."

I stood on unsteady legs, acutely aware of the hundreds of eyes watching my every move. In the gallery above, I could see clusters of students from every major department, their expressions ranging from curious to supportive to openly skeptical. The Fox Den was there in force, with Kieran, Finn, and Jasper occupying an entire row. Even some of my former tutoring students had shown up, their presence both touching and intimidating.

But it was Dylan's steady presence beside me that kept me grounded as I approached the speaking platform.

"Before we begin," Professor Lumina's voice carried clearly through the amphitheater, "I believe the events of this morning have provided crucial context for today's proceedings."

She gestured, and a holographic display materialized above the platform, showing images of the destroyed artifact array and Professor Ember in magical restraints.

"At approximately six this morning," Professor Lumina continued, "Miss Lumina and Mr. Vixen prevented what could have been a mass casualty event by discovering and disabling a weapon system built from stolen NPU artifacts. This system was

designed to force magical bonds between unwilling participants
—a violation of the most fundamental principles of magical
ethics."

Murmurs rippled through the assembled crowd. Several
Winter Court officials shifted uncomfortably in their seats.

"More than that," Professor Lumina's pale eyes fixed on
Professor Arcturus with laser intensity, "the evidence suggests
this was not an isolated incident, but part of a coordinated
campaign to discredit partnership magic research through manufactured crises."

"That," Professor Arcturus said with icy calm, "is a serious
accusation lacking substantive proof."

I knew speaking now could risk everything, but I couldn't stay
silent. Not when the truth was staring us all in the face.

"Is it?" I found myself speaking before I could second-guess
the impulse. "Professor Arcturus, you knew about the stolen artifacts before their theft was officially reported. You've been monitoring Dylan's academic progress since before we met. And your
Winter Court associates had detailed knowledge of NPU's security
systems that would have required inside information."

"Miss Lumina," Professor Arcturus's voice carried a warning
edge, "you are making claims that border on sedition against
established magical authority."

"I'm making observations that border on truth," I shot back,
feeling Dylan's encouraging presence behind me. "You're afraid
students might realize they don't need your permission to be
extraordinary."

The amphitheater had gone dead silent. Even the floating
aurora ribbons seemed to have stilled, as if the magic itself was
holding its breath.

"But most of all," I continued, my voice growing stronger with
each word, "you're afraid that we might prove magical educa-

tion's foundational assumptions are wrong. That cooperation is more powerful than competition. That trust creates better magic than control."

I turned to face the assembled crowd—students, faculty, administrators, and Winter Court officials all watching with rapt attention.

"Partnership magic works," I said, my words carrying clearly through the crystalline acoustics. "Dylan and I have proven it. Not through the unstable bonding you keep warning about, but through collaborative research that enhances individual abilities without compromising personal autonomy."

"Theoretical research," Professor Arcturus interrupted coldly, "conducted without proper oversight or safety protocols."

"Practical research," Dylan said, rising from his seat to join me at the platform, "that prevented a magical disaster this morning."

The air shifted the moment Dylan stepped beside me, our individual magic beginning to hum in shared resonance.

"Dylan Vixen," Professor Arcturus's attention fixed on him with predatory focus, "you stand accused of stealing magical artifacts and conducting unauthorized magical experimentation. How do you answer these charges?"

"I answer," Dylan said with quiet dignity, "that someone with Winter Court resources and detailed knowledge of my magical signature went to extraordinary lengths to frame me for crimes I didn't commit."

He gestured, and the aurora ribbons throughout the amphitheater began to respond to his magic, weaving themselves into complex patterns that spoke to months of dedicated practice and newfound skill.

"I answer that the magical signature found at the theft site was artificially created using recordings made during unauthorized surveillance of partnership magic research."

The light constructs Dylan created were beautiful, precise, and his own—proof that individual magical achievement could be just as spectacular as partnership enhancement.

"But most importantly," Dylan continued, his magic painting the amphitheater in patterns of gold and green, "I answer that I'm exactly where I choose to be. Standing beside someone who makes me want to be better than I am. Someone who taught me that real partnership isn't about magical convenience—it's about choosing to grow together despite imperfection."

He turned to face me, and the look in his green eyes made my heart pound against my ribs. The collective intake of breath from the audience told me they could feel it too—the weight of what was about to be said, the significance of this moment.

"Lyra Lumina," he said, his voice carrying to every corner of the amphitheater, "you are brilliant, courageous, and stubborn enough to fight the Winter Court for what you believe in. You see magic in ways that could revolutionize our understanding of everything. And you make me feel like the smartest, most capable version of myself."

The aurora ribbons were responding to both our magical signatures now, creating patterns that spoke to harmony without dependency, collaboration without loss of individual identity.

"I love you," Dylan said simply. "Not because our magic works well together, but because you do. And if the Winter Court wants to destroy partnership magic research, they'll have to go through both of us."

The words hung in the air like a challenge, like a claim, like a promise that reached every heart in the amphitheater.

"As will I," a voice called from the gallery.

I looked up to see Kieran standing in the Fox Den section, his silver hair catching the dancing lights.

"And me," Finn added, rising beside him.

"Partnership magic saved NPU from disaster this morning," Jasper said, his voice carrying the authority of someone accustomed to leadership. "That doesn't sound dangerous. That sounds like exactly what magical education should be teaching."

One by one, students throughout the gallery began standing. Not just the Fox Den, but water sprites from my tutoring sessions, earth elves from Dylan's study groups, even some of the reindeer shifters who'd initially been skeptical of our research.

Even some professors stood—those who'd remained silent until now, their expressions guarded but resolved.

"Partnership magic isn't just theory," called a familiar voice. I turned to see Marcus rising from his seat, his winter fae heritage evident in the way frost patterns began forming around his feet. "It's practical application of collaborative magical principles that could benefit every student at NPU."

"It's proof," added Sera, my dormitory roommate, "that the best discoveries happen when we're willing to work together instead of competing against each other."

The standing ovation that followed was unlike anything I'd ever experienced. Not just applause, but a collective affirmation that reached beyond academics into something approaching revolution.

"Enough," Professor Arcturus said sharply, his voice cutting through the demonstration. "This is a formal academic hearing, not a popularity contest."

"Isn't it?" Professor Lumina's smile was enigmatic. "Professor Arcturus, magical education exists to serve students, not to control them. When students demonstrate that collaborative approaches produce better results than individual competition, perhaps we should listen."

"The Winter Court position on partnership magic is clear—"

"The Winter Court position," I interrupted, surprising myself with the steel in my voice, "appears to involve theft, conspiracy, and attempted mass murder. Forgive me if I'm not particularly interested in their educational opinions."

Professor Arcturus's expression went dangerously cold. "Miss Lumina, you have just accused the Winter Court of criminal activity before the NPU community."

"I've made factual observations about this morning's events," I corrected. "If those observations happen to reflect poorly on Winter Court activities, perhaps the problem isn't with my analysis."

"You realize," Professor Arcturus said with deadly quiet, "that making such accusations could result in criminal charges against you personally?"

The threat hung in the air like a sword. But before I could respond, Dylan stepped closer, his hand finding mine.

"Then they'll have to charge both of us," he said firmly. "Because we're partners. That means we face whatever comes next together."

The moment our hands touched, our magic responded with joyful harmony. Aurora patterns began painting themselves across the amphitheater's dome, more complex and beautiful than anything we'd achieved during our original partnership bond.

Gasps echoed from the crowd as the aurora intensified—not wild or chaotic, but impossibly synchronized. This was magic beyond partnership bonds, beyond traditional education—born from trust, choice, and belief in each other.

"This," Professor Lumina said with satisfaction, "is what partnership magic actually looks like. Not dependency or instability, but conscious collaboration between equals."

"It's beautiful," someone whispered from the gallery.

"It's impossible," someone else added with wonder.

"It's everything magical education should be teaching," Professor Lumina concluded. "Miss Lumina, your research privileges are hereby fully reinstated. Mr. Vixen, all charges against you are formally dismissed. And partnership magic research is approved for expanded study under proper academic protocols."

The roar of approval from the gallery was deafening. But I barely heard it, because Dylan was looking at me with an expression that made everything else fade.

"So," he said with that familiar mischievous grin, "does this mean we're officially the NPU poster couple for academic rebellion?"

"I think," I said, standing on my toes to bring our faces closer together, "it means we're exactly what we choose to be."

"And what do we choose to be?"

"Partners," I said simply. "In research, in magic, in whatever comes next."

"Always?"

"Always."

"This isn't just love," Dylan whispered, his forehead touching mine. "This is a claim. Of my choice, my future—with you."

When Dylan kissed me this time, it wasn't hesitant or questioning. It was a declaration that reached every corner of the amphitheater. The aurora displays that bloomed around us painted the crystal dome in patterns that spoke to harmony achieved through choice rather than chance.

And as the Spring Equinox sun reached its zenith above NPU, casting rainbow patterns through the aurora light, I realized that sometimes the most powerful magic wasn't something you found by accident.

It was something you built, day by day, choice by choice, heartbeat by heartbeat, with someone who made you believe that anything was possible.

The Winter Court could keep their control. We had something better.

We had each other.

As the formal hearing concluded and students began flowing down from the gallery to congratulate us, I caught sight of Professor Arcturus making his way toward the exit with swift, sharp movements. His pale eyes met mine across the crowd, and I saw something in them that made my stomach clench with unease.

In that glare, I saw calculation, not defeat. Arcturus wasn't finished—he was already planning his next move.

But looking around at the faces surrounding us—Dylan's friends from the Fox Den, my former tutoring students, professors who'd chosen to support academic freedom over institutional control—I realized something important.

We weren't fighting this battle alone anymore.

Partnership magic had given us more than just academic vindication. It had given us community, chosen family, and the kind of support that came from people who believed in the same vision of what magical education could become.

"Think they'll let us build a formal partnership magic lab?" Dylan asked, grinning as he accepted congratulations from the celebrating crowd.

"They won't have a choice," I replied, feeling more certain than I'd ever felt about anything.

"Ready for what comes next?" Dylan asked, his arm still wrapped around my waist.

"With you?" I smiled up at him. "I'm ready for everything. Because we weren't just rebuilding magic anymore—we were building a future."

Because whatever the Winter Court threw at us next, whatever challenges awaited partnership magic research, whatever obstacles stood between us and the future we wanted to build—we'd face them the same way we'd faced everything else.

Together.

And that, I was beginning to understand, was the most powerful magic of all.

CHAPTER TWENTY-ONE
BALANCE RESTORED

DYLAN

The Reindeer Games arena buzzed with anticipation—the kind born of rivalry, not spells. Three weeks had passed since the Spring Equinox hearing, and NPU's annual athletic competition had transformed from a simple sporting event into something approaching a celebration of everything we'd fought to defend.

Partnership magic demonstrations were now part of the official curriculum. Students from different magical backgrounds were openly collaborating on research projects. Even the Winter Court representatives who'd remained on campus after Professor Arcturus's departure seemed resigned to the new reality.

But right now, none of that mattered. Because I was about to compete in the Aerial Agility Challenge—the one event I'd been dreaming of since freshman year—and for the first time in my life, I wasn't planning to cheat.

"You're really not going to use any illusion magic?" Kieran asked for the third time as we stood at the starting line. His silver hair was pulled back in a practical ponytail, and his winter wolf energy hummed with anticipation for his own event later.

"Not even a little misdirection spell?" Finn added, checking the straps on his practice harness. "Dylan, this is the Games. Everyone expects fox shifters to be clever about the rules."

I looked around the arena, taking in the obstacle course that would test every aspect of aerial maneuvering—speed, precision, teamwork, and adaptability. Floating platforms shifted position unpredictably. Ribbon gates that required perfect coordination between multiple flyers. Challenge segments that could only be completed through collaborative magical applications.

"That's exactly why I'm not doing it," I said, surprising myself with how certain I sounded. "Everyone expects fox shifters to win through tricks and loopholes. I want to win because I'm actually good at this."

"Dylan," Jasper's concern was genuine, "this is your shot at proving yourself to the Games recruiters. If you don't place—"

"Then I don't place," I interrupted. "But at least I'll know I earned whatever happens."

The truth was, these past weeks of training had taught me something important about myself. Working with Lyra hadn't just improved my magic—it had shown me what I was capable of when I stopped looking for shortcuts and started trusting my actual abilities.

"Dylan Vixen," the Games announcer called through the arena's magical amplification system, "you're up for the individual qualifying round."

I shifted into fox form, feeling the familiar rush as my magic settled into the sleek, efficient shape built for speed and agility. My rust-colored fur caught the arena lighting, and I could hear cheers from the Fox Den section of the stands.

But the cheer that mattered most came from the faculty

observation box, where Lyra sat with Professor Lumina and several other Light Wing instructors. She'd been invited to watch from the VIP section as part of her new role as the Light Apprenticeship program's youngest-ever inductee.

When our eyes met across the arena, Lyra's smile was bright enough to power the entire magical lighting system. She raised her hand in a small wave, and I felt that familiar flutter of connection—not magical partnership, but something deeper. The certainty that someone believed in me completely.

Time to show them what Dylan Vixen can really do.

The starting bell chimed, and I launched myself into the course.

The first section tested pure speed—a series of floating rings that required precise navigation at maximum velocity. I dove through them with the fluid grace that came from months of systematic training rather than innate talent. No shortcuts, no illusions to make the rings appear larger than they were. Just my own reflexes and the confidence that came from actual preparation.

The second section was where most competitors stumbled: collaborative magical casting while maintaining aerial precision. Teams of three had to maintain formation while creating combined light displays that met specific technical requirements.

"Vixen!" called Marcus Chen, a wind elemental from my Magical Theory class. "You're with us!"

I joined Marcus and Sera Brightwater, a water sprite who'd been in several of my study groups. We'd never trained together as a team, but we'd spent enough time working on joint projects to understand each other's magical styles.

"Aurora pattern, synchronized spiral formation?" Sera suggested as we approached the casting zone.

"I can provide the light framework," I said, already reaching for the advanced techniques Lyra had taught me. "Marcus, can you handle the wind currents to maintain our positioning?"

"On it."

What followed was the kind of collaborative magic I'd never thought possible without formal partnership bonds. Marcus's wind magic created perfect atmospheric conditions for my light constructs, while Sera's water manipulation added prismatic effects that turned our aurora display into something genuinely beautiful.

We moved through the course like a crew operating by instinct and trust rather than rehearsed steps—not because magic was forcing us into harmony, but because we'd chosen to work together. When we completed the required pattern and crossed the finish line in perfect formation, the arena erupted in cheers.

"Team Collaboration score: 94 out of 100," the announcer declared. "Individual technique scores: Marcus Chen, 89. Sera Brightwater, 91. Dylan Vixen, 96."

Ninety-six. My highest individual score in any Games event, ever.

As we landed on the arena floor, Sera grabbed my arm with excitement. "Dylan, that light magic was incredible! How did you learn to cast aurora patterns while maintaining flight formation?"

"Someone taught me that the best magic happens when you're willing to work for it," I said, catching sight of Lyra in the observation box. She was on her feet, applauding with genuine pride that made my chest ache with affection.

"Well, whoever they are, they should be proud," Marcus said with a grin. "That was partnership magic without the partnership bonds. Pure collaborative skill."

The final section tested adaptive problem-solving—obstacles that shifted unpredictably, forcing real-time adaptation. This was where fox shifter versatility traditionally gave us an advantage, but it was also where most of us relied too heavily on illusion magic to compensate for poor planning.

I approached each challenge methodically, using the systematic thinking Lyra had drilled into me during our tutoring sessions. When the floating platforms shifted mid-flight, I adjusted my trajectory based on mathematical calculations rather than magical shortcuts. When the ribbon gates changed color to signal new navigation requirements, I read the visual cues correctly instead of casting spells to make them appear simpler.

By the time I completed the final segment—a precision landing that required threading between moving obstacles—I was exhausted but exhilarated. For the first time in my academic career, I'd given my absolute best effort without relying on tricks or shortcuts.

"Individual Adaptive Challenge score: Dylan Vixen, 93 out of 100. Overall Games standing: second place in the Aerial Agility division."

Second place had never felt this satisfying—because I'd earned every point of it.

As I shifted back to human form and caught my breath, I realized something fundamental had changed. This wasn't just about proving myself worthy of the Vixen name anymore. This was about proving to myself that I was exactly who I chose to be.

"Dylan!" Lyra's voice carried across the arena as she made her way down from the observation box. She moved with the controlled grace that had first caught my attention, but now her composed demeanor was offset by genuine excitement. "That was amazing! The collaborative aurora sequence, the adaptive navigation—"

I swept her into my arms, spinning her around as she laughed with delight. "Did you see that? I actually earned it. No illusions, no shortcuts, just—"

"Just you," she finished, her pale eyes bright with pride. "Dylan, that was partnership magic at its finest. Not because of bonds or magical enhancement, but because you trusted your teammates and they trusted you back."

She touched my face gently, her expression soft with something deeper than academic pride. "I watched you up there, and I could see how different you looked. Confident in a way that came from knowing your abilities, not just hoping they'd be enough."

"I felt like I belonged up there," I admitted. "For the first time in my life, I wasn't pretending to be capable. I actually was."

"I always believed in your potential," she whispered. "Now you believe it too."

The simple truth of her words made my throat tight with emotion.

"We make a pretty good team," I said, setting her down but keeping my arms around her waist.

"The best team," she agreed. "Though I have to admit, I was holding my breath during that final precision segment."

"You? Worried about mathematical calculations? Lyra, I had every trajectory mapped out before I even started the approach."

"You've been paying attention during our study sessions," she said with playful surprise.

"I've been paying attention to my brilliant girlfriend," I corrected, earning a blush that made her even more beautiful.

"Speaking of brilliant," Finn's voice interrupted as the Fox Den crowd descended on us, "when did Dylan Vixen become someone who earns second place through actual skill instead of creative rule interpretation?"

"About the time he started working with someone who

wouldn't let him get away with taking shortcuts," I said, squeezing Lyra's hand.

"Well, whatever you did, it worked," Kieran said with genuine admiration. "That collaborative sequence was the best thing I've seen in the Games all year. You looked like you actually belonged up there."

Jasper clapped me on the shoulder with the kind of pack pride that made my chest tight with emotion. "Second place in Aerial Agility. Dylan, that's going to get attention from some serious Games recruiters."

"More importantly," Lyra added quietly, "it's going to get attention from students who want to learn what collaborative magic really looks like."

She was right. Already, I could see clusters of younger students watching our group with obvious interest. Not because we'd pulled off some spectacular trick, but because we'd demonstrated that different magical backgrounds could work together to achieve something none of us could have managed alone.

"Hey," Marcus Chen approached with Sera and several other students from our collaborative team. "Dylan, we were talking, and we want to ask you something."

"What's that?"

"Would you be interested in forming an official Partnership Magic study group? Nothing formal, just students who want to explore collaborative casting techniques."

I looked around at the faces watching me with genuine respect rather than the amused tolerance I'd grown used to from my classmates. These weren't students looking for entertainment or someone to help them bend the rules. These were people who'd seen what partnership magic could accomplish and wanted to be part of something meaningful.

"I'd be honored," I said. "But I should probably mention that my girlfriend is the real expert on partnership magic theory. I just provide the practical application."

"We'd love to have both of you," Sera said eagerly. "If Lyra's willing."

"Try to keep me away," Lyra said with a smile that transformed her entire face. "Though I should warn you, I take magical education very seriously."

"Good," Marcus said with a grin. "We're not looking for easy answers. We want to learn how to do this right."

As the conversation continued around us, I found myself marveling at how completely my life had changed in a single semester. Six months ago, I'd been a mediocre student coasting on charm and family connections, desperate to prove myself worthy of the Vixen name through pranks and clever shortcuts.

Now I was standing in the Reindeer Games arena, having earned second place through genuine skill, surrounded by classmates who respected my abilities and wanted to learn from my experiences. More than that, I was partnered with someone who challenged me to be better while loving me exactly as I was.

And according to the Games recruiter who'd approached me after the scores were announced, I was being considered for a summer internship with the Elite Aerial Corps—a position that had never been offered to a sophomore before.

"You know," I said to Lyra as the crowd began to disperse, "when this semester started, I thought the Games were about proving I was good enough to live up to family expectations."

"And now?"

"Now I know they're about proving to myself that I'm exactly who I choose to be."

Lyra's smile was radiant. "Which is?"

"Someone who earns what he gets. Someone who builds people up instead of tearing them down. Someone who's brave enough to trust his partner completely." I brushed a strand of dark hair from her face. "Someone worthy of being loved by the most brilliant woman at NPU."

"Dylan," she said softly, "you've always been worthy of that. You just needed to recognize it yourself."

As the arena lighting shifted to accommodate the next event, I realized she was absolutely right. The partnership magic, the academic success, even the Games placement—none of it had made me worthy of love. It had simply helped me recognize worth I'd possessed all along.

"So," I said, taking her hand as we headed toward the celebration area where our friends were gathering, "ready to show everyone what the Light Apprenticeship program's star student can do with aurora displays?"

"Actually," Lyra said with a mischievous smile I'd never seen before, "I was thinking we could collaborate on something special. A little demonstration of what partnership magic looks like when it's built on choice rather than chance."

"What did you have in mind?"

"Trust me?"

Looking into her eyes—brilliant, determined, and sparkling with the kind of creative mischief she'd learned from spending time with fox shifters—I realized that was the easiest question anyone had ever asked me.

"Always."

As we joined our friends under the arena's glowing lights, surrounded by laughter and celebration and the kind of community neither of us had expected to find, I knew with absolute certainty that this was exactly where I belonged.

Not because magic had chosen it for us, but because we'd chosen it for ourselves.

CHAPTER TWENTY-TWO
A BRIGHTER PATH

LYRA

The Spring Festival had transformed NPU's main courtyard into something from a fairy tale. Magic kept the mountain night warm, lanterns drifting like stars amid ribbons of aurora light that wove between the trees, shifting through every color imaginable as they responded to the collective magical energy of hundreds of celebrating students.

But the most beautiful sight wasn't the magical decorations— it was Dylan, standing at the edge of the dance floor with his hands extended toward me, his green eyes bright with mischief and affection.

"Dance with me?" he asked, his voice carrying easily over the music that seemed to emanate from the very air around us.

"I should warn you," I said, taking his hands anyway, "I've never been particularly graceful at social dancing."

"Good thing I've never been particularly conventional at anything," Dylan replied with that grin that still made my pulse quicken. "Trust me?"

"Always."

He led me onto the makeshift dance floor that had been created in the courtyard's center, where dozens of other couples moved to music that felt like liquid starlight. I'd expected to feel self-conscious, aware of all the eyes that might be watching NPU's most infamous partnership magic couple, but the moment Dylan's arms wrapped around me, the festival noise dimmed to a distant hum.

"See?" he murmured as we found our rhythm. "Sometimes the best magic happens when you stop worrying about perfection."

As we moved together, our combined magical signatures began responding to the music—and to each other. Tiny orbs of light started materializing around us, hovering at shoulder height and pulsing in time with the melody. But these weren't the structured, controlled displays I typically created. They were organic, playful, touched with Dylan's chaotic creativity.

Light and mischief, perfectly balanced.

"Dylan," I said softly, watching as more couples began to notice our magical accompaniment, "we're drawing attention."

"We're creating beauty," he corrected, spinning me in a move that made our light orbs dance in complex spirals around us. "Besides, when have we ever been subtle?"

He was right. From our first disaster of a tutoring session to our public vindication at the Spring Equinox hearing, subtlety had never been our strength. But maybe that was okay. Maybe some discoveries were meant to be celebrated openly.

As I looked into his eyes, feeling the steady warmth of our connection, something profound settled in my chest. For years, I'd carried the weight of Professor Lumina's expectations, the legacy of my parents' research, the pressure to prove myself worthy of their academic lineage. But this—partnership magic born from choice rather than obligation—this was mine. Ours. A mission we'd discovered together.

Partnership magic wasn't just theory anymore. It was the path we'd chosen to walk.

"Always," Dylan whispered, the promise written in his eyes. "Magic or no magic."

When he dipped me dramatically enough to make me laugh, our light orbs intensified, creating a private aurora that painted everything in shades of silver and rose gold.

"Lyra?" he said quietly as he pulled me back upright.

"Yes?"

"I keep thinking about what Professor Lumina said. About partnership magic being the future of magical education."

I pulled back slightly to meet his eyes. "And?"

"I think we're just getting started," Dylan continued, his voice growing more excited. "The study group, the collaborative research, the way younger students are already asking to learn partnership techniques—what if this is bigger than just us? What if we're part of something that could change everything?"

The idea sent a thrill through me that had nothing to do with romance and everything to do with possibility. "A revolution in magical education?"

"A revolution in how people think about magic, period." Dylan's grin was infectious. "Lyra, what if instead of competing against each other, students learned to enhance each other? What if collaboration became the foundation instead of the exception?"

"It would require completely restructuring the curriculum," I said, my mind already racing through the implications. "New assessment methods, different teaching approaches, faculty training programs—"

"It would require people like us to prove it works," Dylan

interrupted gently. "People willing to show that partnership magic isn't just possible, it's better."

Around us, the Spring Festival continued its magical celebration, but I found myself imagining something different. A version of NPU where students like Dylan didn't struggle alone with magic designed for collaboration. Where brilliant minds weren't isolated by competition but brought together by shared purpose.

"Are you asking if I want to spend the rest of our time at NPU being magical education revolutionaries?" I asked.

"I'm asking if you want to spend the rest of our time at NPU—and maybe beyond—building something extraordinary together."

The light orbs around us pulsed brighter, responding to the surge of excitement flowing between us. Other couples had stopped dancing to watch our impromptu display, but for once, I didn't mind the attention.

"Yes," I said without hesitation. "Absolutely yes."

Dylan's answering smile was radiant enough to rival our magical display. He spun me again, laughing with pure joy as our aurora grew more spectacular.

But the magic between us fractured as a sharp cry pierced the celebration.

"What's happening?" I asked, trying to see through the crowd turning toward the festival's main entrance.

"I don't know, but—" Dylan started, then stopped as a figure burst through the gathered students.

It was a girl I didn't recognize—tiny even by sprite standards, with silver-white hair that caught the festival lights like spun moonbeams. She was clearly in distress, her pale blue skin flushed with magical exhaustion, and she was being followed by—

"Is that Rowan Blackthorn?" Dylan asked, his voice tight with surprise.

I followed his gaze to see a tall, dark-haired young man

emerging from the crowd. He moved like a storm bottled into human form—calm on the surface, but with something dangerous coiled beneath. Even at a distance, there was something unsettling about his magical presence that made other students unconsciously step aside.

"Who's Rowan Blackthorn?" I asked.

"Winter witch family. Very old bloodline, very powerful, and very..." Dylan paused, searching for the right word. "Cursed isn't right, but there are stories. Bad luck seems to follow them around."

The tiny sprite stumbled and nearly fell before catching herself against the fountain. As Rowan reached her, the air around them suddenly sparked with chaotic energy—dark magic clashing against ice-bright power in a way that made nearby students cry out in alarm.

Stone cracked. Festival lanterns exploded in showers of harmless sparks.

"We need to help," I said, already moving. "That binding is going critical."

"Lyra, I don't think—"

But I was already running, our light orbs trailing behind me as I approached the pair. Up close, the sprite looked even more distressed, her magical aura flickering like a candle in a hurricane.

"Are you alright?" I asked gently.

The girl looked up at me with eyes the color of winter frost, and I saw recognition flash across her features. "You're Lyra Lumina. The partnership magic researcher."

"I am. And you are?"

"Ivy Snowfall," she said, her voice barely above a whisper. "I'm sorry, I didn't mean to disrupt the festival. There was an accident during practice, and our magic got tangled somehow, and now I can't—"

"You can't separate," Rowan finished grimly, staying carefully out of arm's reach. "And it's my fault."

Another surge of unstable energy crackled between them, this time strong enough to make the fountain's crystal base groan ominously.

"How long ago did this happen?" I asked urgently.

"About an hour," Ivy said, swaying on her feet. "We came looking for help, but everyone said you and Dylan were the partnership magic experts, and—"

"Dylan," I called, not taking my eyes off the increasingly dangerous magical field around the two students. "I need you here. Now."

He appeared at my side instantly, taking in the situation with quick assessment. "Magical binding gone wrong?"

"Very wrong." I gestured toward the dark energy crackling between Ivy and Rowan. "If we don't stabilize this soon, the backlash could hurt everyone here."

I looked at the two students—Ivy, brilliant and determined despite her exhaustion; Rowan, powerful and haunted by whatever family legacy had led to this moment—and felt that familiar surge of protective determination.

This was exactly what Dylan and I had been discussing. Partnership magic going wrong because students didn't have proper training, proper support, proper understanding of what they were attempting.

"We're going to help you," I said firmly. "Both of you. But first, we need to get somewhere private where we can work without endangering everyone else."

"The Observatory?" Dylan suggested.

"Perfect." I turned back to Ivy and Rowan. "Can you make it that far?"

"I think so," Ivy said, though she looked anything but certain.

"I'll make sure she can," Rowan said quietly, and for the first time, he stepped closer to her. The moment he did, some of the chaotic energy settled—not resolved, but contained.

As we made our way through the festival crowd toward the Lumina Wing, I caught Dylan's hand in mine. Our light orbs had faded, but the warmth between us remained steady and sure.

"So much for a quiet end to the semester," he said with rueful amusement.

"Since when have we ever done anything quietly?" I replied.

"Good point." Dylan squeezed my fingers gently. "Though I have to say, if we're going to start our magical education revolution, helping two students with a dangerous binding situation is a pretty dramatic beginning."

I looked back at Ivy and Rowan, noting the way they moved together despite the obvious tension between them—drawn by magical necessity but fighting the connection at every step.

"I think," I said quietly, "our revolution just found its first official case study."

"Partnership magic for unwilling partners?"

"Exactly. Proving collaboration can thrive even when it starts with conflict." I smiled, feeling the familiar thrill of a new theoretical challenge. "This could be what we need to show that partnership magic works even for people who think they're incompatible."

"Assuming we can figure out how to help them without making things worse."

"Dylan," I said, watching as Rowan steadied Ivy when she stumbled again, his touch gentle despite his obvious reluctance, "look at them. Really look."

He followed my gaze, and I saw understanding dawn in his expression. Whatever magical accident had bound these two students together, their energy signatures were already beginning to adapt to each other. Ivy's flickering magic was gaining stability from Rowan's steady presence, while his dark power was being softened by her light touch.

"They're not incompatible at all," Dylan said with wonder. "They're just scared."

"And if we can help them work through the fear, we might prove that partnership magic can bloom from the most unlikely beginnings."

As we reached the Lumina Wing, I realized that Dylan had been absolutely right earlier. We were just getting started. Tomorrow, I'd propose a formal partnership magic mentoring program to Professor Lumina. We'd turn the Observatory into a proper training center. We'd show NPU—and the magical world—that collaboration could be taught, nurtured, and celebrated.

But tonight, we had two students who needed our help.

And whatever came next—whether it was revolutionizing magical education, mentoring the next generation of partnership mages, or simply continuing to build the most extraordinary connection I'd ever imagined—we'd face it the same way we'd faced everything else.

We'd chosen this path—uncertain, challenging, and full of impossible questions. But we'd chosen it together.

The question was: could we help Ivy and Rowan find the same kind of trust?

Looking at the two students following us through the castle corridors—one tiny and fierce, the other powerful and burdened by shadows—I had the feeling our next semester was going to be very interesting indeed.

Time to find out if partnership magic could save two people who were convinced they were meant to walk through the world alone.

The End.

Did you enjoy *Sophomore Solstice*?

Please consider leaving a review on Goodreads, Bookbub or your favorite retailer. Reviews help me reach new readers.

Read *Junior Jinx* the next book in the **North Pole University** series.

Join my Newsletter for weekly writing updates, exclusive content, new releases, sales, and promotions.

ABOUT THE AUTHOR

Positive, uplifting books and stories.

Marie-Hélène Lebeault is the author of *The Evers Series, Clarity Castle, What Happens Next? Readers Decide Which Story Becomes a Book,* the *Blood Magick Trilogy, Holiday Shifters, Ghost Stories, Defenders of the Realm, Utopia, Chronicles of the Starborne Cadets, Legends Reborn,* as well as a series of picture books called Fairy Grandmother. She lives in Canada with her grown children.

www.mhlebeault.com

Follow on Social Media, she'd love to hear from you!

facebook.com/mhlebeaultauthor

x.com/mhlebeault

instagram.com/mhlebeault

amazon.com/author/mhlebeault

bookbub.com/authors/marie-helene-lebeault

goodreads.com/mhlebeault

linkedin.com/in/mhlebeault

tiktok.com/@mhlebeaultauthor

ALSO BY THE AUTHOR

North Pole University - NA Paranormal Romance

Holiday Shifters

Freshman Frost

Sophomore Solstice

Junior Jinx

Senior Spark

Wedded Bliss

Mistletoe Misfits

Legends Reborn - NA Fairytale Retellings

A Curse of Snow and Ash

A Curse of Thorns and Slumber

A Curse of Glass and Shadows

A Curse of Scars and Silver

The Chronicles of the Starborne Cadets - YA Space Opera

Confluence of Destinies (Prequel)

Stars Beyond Realms

Shadows of Orion

Echoes of the Void

The Nebula's Heart

The Starborne Paradox

Defenders of the Realm - YA Epic Fantasy

A Journey to Power

The Quest for the Emerald Rattleback

A Summer of Discovery

The Quest for the Sacred Tree

A Summer of Opposites

The Quest for the Phantom Feather

A Summer of Courage

The Quest for the Kraken's Ink

A Summer of Destiny

The Quest for the Cursed Mirrors

A Summer of Unity

Defenders of the Realm - Special Edition Hardcover Set

The Evers Series - YA Science Fantasy

The Ancestors' Key

The Academy

The Time Walker

The World Jumper

5th Anniversary Edition Omnibus

The Traveler's Handbook

The Lost Key

Blood Magick Trilogy - YA Urban Fantasy

The Blood Mage

Blood Magick

Blood Legacy

Extended Edition Omnibus

Standalones

Clarity Castle

What Happens Next?

Ghost Stories

Echoes of Tomorrow

Utopia

Picture Books

Fairy Grandmother: Millie Goes to Antarctica

Fairy Grandmother: Millie Goes to the North Pole

Fairy Grandmother: Millie Goes to China

Fairy Grandmother: Millie Goes to Africa

(Also available in French, Spanish, German, and Italian)

www.ingramcontent.com/pod-product-compliance
Lightning Source LLC
Chambersburg PA
CBHW050409260626
47156CB00003B/939